Return of the Buffalo Hunter

Wade Guthrie is a menacing man. Turning away from the life of a Texas Ranger after murdering the entire family of a wanted man, he became an outlaw with a deadly gang by his side. The gruesome group get wind of a man known only to most as O'Brien. A buffalo hunter and a trapper, he just wants a quiet life without looking for trouble… But he didn't expect his wife, Sarah, to have a terrifying experience with two of Guthrie's men! That encounter, following a string of deaths at a Wells Fargo depot, leads the local sheriff to request O'Brien's help. Unexpectedly, O'Brien must assume the role of a lawman and carry iron against a dangerous foe. Will he be able to get to grips with this man without a conscience?

Return of the Buffalo Hunter

Ralph Hayes

A Black Horse Western

ROBERT HALE

© Ralph Hayes 2020
First published in Great Britain in 2020

ISBN 978-0-7198-3141-6

The Crowood Press
The Stable Block
Crowood Lane
Ramsbury
Marlborough
Wiltshire SN8 2HR

www.bhwesterns.com

Robert Hale is an imprint
of The Crowood Press

The right of Ralph Hayes to be identified as
author of this work has been asserted by him
in accordance with the Copyright, Designs
and Patents Act 1988

Typeset by
Simon and Sons ITES Services Pvt Ltd
Printed and bound in Great Britain by
4Bind Ltd, Stevenage, SG1 2XT

ONE

Wade Guthrie turned from the smoldering fireplace where he had been silently standing to face the other three men in the one-room cabin. They had all been waiting patiently for him to speak.

'You understand, of course, that we'll have to kill everyone we find there.'

He was a rather tall man, in his late thirties, with dark hair and a badly broken nose. A deadly looking Schofield .45 hung menacingly on his right hip. He read dark poetry, and there was something missing inside Guthrie, something that defined a whole human being, and every man in the room knew it, and as hard-bitten as they all were, they were wary of it.

'Masks wouldn't help,' he added indifferently, as if the issue wasn't important to him. 'The depot agent knows me.'

Two of his audience sat at a crude kitchen table, and a third stood across the room against a double bunk. He was a Lakota half-breed known only as Skin Walker. About Guthrie's age, he was slim and muscular, and wore a buckskin tunic over dungarees. He believed he was descended from an evil Lakota god and was endowed with supernatural powers. He prayed irregularly and very privately to that god, and was a stone-cold killer not unlike Guthrie.

'Then it is written,' he offered in his deep, whispery voice.

At the table, a brawny man with a heavily lined face studied Guthrie for a moment. His name was Avery Morgan, and he had been with Guthrie longer than the others, and was always just a bit careful with him. Guthrie considered him to be his top man. He was a little older than Guthrie and had dishwater-colored eyes. He was also a distant relative of Guthrie, but didn't admit that to anyone who didn't already know it. Like Guthrie, he was wanted for murder in other places.

'The more killings we leave behind us, the more attention we get from the law.'

Guthrie scowled at him. 'You going soft on me, Avery?' He had standing with the others because he had been a Texas Ranger for a short time, when Rangers were more interested in a recruit's ability to shoot than what his morals were. He had been fired over a year ago for killing the entire family of a wanted man, without any justification. Shortly afterwards he had taken up outlawry to make his way in life.

Morgan did not reply to Guthrie's remark, but the other man at the table, a fellow named Simon Tate, laughed in his throat. 'Hell, take them all out. I don't care who's there.' He was a very short man

6

with dwarfish characteristics, such as thick, bowed legs and heavy shoulders. He stood just chest high to Guthrie. He had an odd personality with a quick temper, which he never showed to Guthrie. At a young age he had killed his own stepfather with a baseball bat.

Guthrie looked back at his sidekick Morgan. 'I don't worry about the law around here. There's just that sheriff in Birney Pass who doesn't know where the trigger is on that Colt he carries. What's important is that nobody can identify us when it's over. At Wells Fargo or anywhere around there.'

'I'm fine with that, Wade,' Morgan finally agreed. 'Incidentally. When I was in Birney Pass the other day, that Sheriff Purvis was standing out on the street talking with some big man in rawhides, I think he called him O'Brien. You suppose Purvis is trying to hire a deputy? They looked to be in serious palaver.'

'I don't care if he hires a whole posse,' Guthrie grunted, turning back to stoke the fire with a poker. 'I've already killed one sheriff and his half-wit deputy, over in Laramie. I hope he does come after us. I'd like to notch up another lawman.' But now Skin Walker spoke up again. 'Wait a minute.' He turned to Morgan.

'Did you say Purvis mentioned the name O'Brien?' Morgan nodded. 'So what?'

Walker closed his eyes for a moment. He did that sometimes and they never asked why. 'If he is with Purvis, it is a bad sign. He is the White Lakota.'

'The what?' Guthrie said impatiently.

7

'I will kill a badger and eat its liver. It will protect us against him. There is nothing to be concerned about.'

'I'm not concerned,' Guthrie frowned. 'Have you been drinking, Walker?'

'You're a white face. You wouldn't understand. You see, he is special to the tribes of the Lakota. The story goes that he was born full-grown in a bear cave near Ogalalla, and that he is a creation of the Thunderbird.'

'For God's sake,' side-kick Morgan mumbled.

'No, wait,' the tall dwarf put in; 'I've heard about this man. The Indians think he can't be killed with a bullet.'

Skin Walker looked at the hand-rived ceiling. 'There are stories about him. In a saloon in Wichita he walked through a hail of gunfire by a drifter and beat him to death with his bare hands.'

Morgan shook his head. 'And you believe that?'

Walker shrugged. 'It is only what I heard. He used to hunt buffalo.'

Guthrie shook his head. 'Can we get back to business here? We have important things to discuss. I want to do this Thursday, in two days. Will all of you be ready to ride?'

There was general assent in the room. Simon Tate the half-dwarf reached subconsciously to his side and laid his hand gently on a protruding Starr .44 revolver there.

'This stage depot is on the trail between Birney Pass and Scottville,' Guthrie went on, 'and I want to be there before noon, in between stage stops. The agent is a man called Seger, and he lives there. There might be a family member or two. There's no way of knowing if they will be there.'

Morgan looked up at him soberly.

'I'm told Seger will have a stash of silver there to be put aboard the afternoon stage. Going to some bank in Boulder. He keeps it in a small safe. Seger will not be touched till the safe is open. When we have the silver...'

The door of the cabin swung open and a young man stood there. All eyes turned to him.

'Wade. Boys,' he grinned sheepishly. He was the last member of Guthrie's rather hastily assembled gang, and Guthrie was already irritated with his independent nature, and wondering if he was really dependable. He was Eben Garrett, only nineteen years old, but with a nickname of 'One Shot' because he had already killed four men in saloon brawls requiring just one shot from the Tranter .38 that now hung ostentatiously on his hip. He was blondish, and had done trick shooting in a Wild West show, and that was why Guthrie had hired him.

Guthrie leaned against the wall beside the fireplace, and took a deep breath in. 'Where the hell have you been, boy?' he growled. 'Maybe you forgot I said nine a.m.'

The lanky youngster was not intimidated. He walked to the table and sat on a third chair near Morgan. 'Sorry, Wade. I was with a girl.' An apologetic grin. 'I couldn't pull her off me.'

The short, wizened Tate grunted out a laugh, but everybody else was silent, watching Guthrie's reaction.

Guthrie walked over to the table and stood over Garrett. 'So you enjoyed yourself, Eben?'

'I always know that in advance,' Garrett grinned. He had what Guthrie considered an unnatural appetite for almost any young woman who was thrown into his path.

'Where did you meet her?' Guthrie now said pleasantly.

The grin slid off Garrett's face, 'Why, over in Scottville. In the saloon there.' Watching Guthrie's face closely.

'Do you take any of this seriously, Eben? I mean, the things we're doing here? The things we're going to be doing?'

'Well, of course, Wade. You know how much I respect you.'

Guthrie swung an open hand at Garrett and slapped him so hard he almost lost his balance on the chair. His hand automatically went for the Tranter on his belt. But before he could draw, Guthrie's Schofield was snug up against his nose, in a move his eye couldn't follow.

Garrett sucked his breath in. 'Jesus, Wade!' Breathlessly.

'You start taking this seriously or you're gone,' Guthrie said quietly, without a hint of emotion.

Not knowing what he meant by that, Garrett swallowed hard. 'Sure.' His cheek burning hotly. 'I got it, Wade.'

Skin Walker grunted out a small laugh in his throat, and Morgan privately shook his head at him.

Guthrie had turned back to the others. 'I'm going to make all of you a lot of money. But I call all the shots. All you have to do is listen carefully to everything I tell you. And perform. Any questions?'

The room was silent.

'Good. Now we're going to approach this like a military operation. From now on till I say otherwise, we're all sleeping here. Avery, bring in some cots. And some provisions from Birney Pass.'

Morgan nodded. 'I'll get at it today.'

'I've got big plans for us after the Wells Fargo job. Avery. What did you say the name of that hunter was you saw with Sheriff Purvis?'

Morgan frowned quizzically. 'O'Brien. Why?'

Guthrie stared across the room. 'What you said about them talking seriously. The hunter would be different from Purvis. He could cause us trouble when we least want it. After we're through with this Thursday, I want you to find out where he lives, and take him out.'

Morgan smiled, and nodded his understanding. 'Take the kid with you,' Guthrie added.

Garrett's face showed surprise, but he didn't respond.

'Well, that's it. Go with Avery for supplies, Tate,' he said to the dwarf-like man at the table. You can run your errands, boys, but discuss everything with me first. Everything.'

Again, silence.

11

All went well until Thursday, and just after dawn on that day, the five outlaws rode off to the stage depot.

It was a very warm summer day, and the temperature was already high by mid-morning, when they arrived at the depot.

The five reined in outside the low, rambling building and sat their mounts quietly, looking the place over. 'This is it?' the short, squat Tate said with ill-hidden disdain. His saddle grunted under his weight.

'Don't let appearances fool you,' Guthrie assured them. 'This line takes in a lot of bank stuff.'

They all dismounted at a hitching rail. 'Remember what I said,' Guthrie then announced. 'We don't want witnesses.'

A couple of moments later they filed through the big open door of the depot. It was quiet inside. They were in a large waiting room and office combined, with a couple rows of benches centrally. On one side wall was a bank of file cabinets, and on the wall to their left were two desks. The depot agent Seger was sitting at the larger of the two desks, and looked up in surprise at their entry. He was a small man wearing a green visor and sleeve garters.

'There's no stage through here for three hours, gentlemen. But feel free to sit and wait.'

Guthrie walked over to him. 'We're not here to ride your coaches, Seger,' he said pleasantly.

Seger stood up, and still had to look up several inches at Guthrie. 'Why, it's Mr. Gunter, ain't it?'

'Guthrie.'

'Oh, of course.' An apologetic grin. 'I think you rode with us to Boulder a little while back.'

The other four men were wandering around the room, looking it over. Simon Tate had found the free-standing safe in a corner, and was standing in front of it, studying it closely. 'What company built this chicken coop?' he called to Seger across the room.

Seger turned from Guthrie to frown at Tate. 'Can I help you boys with anything?' Speaking to Guthrie again.

Guthrie sighed. "The fact is, Seger, we're here to relieve you of the silver that was just delivered to your safe over there.'

Seger's face changed dramatically. 'What?'

'Come on,' Guthrie purred at him. 'I know it came on time. Nobody is going to blame you for giving it over to armed men. Just open the safe for us and we'll take what's there and be on our way. Nobody will get hurt. Is your assistant here?'

'Why, yes. Ned's out back. But I can't do what you ask.' 'Call him. Anybody else?'

Seger's mouth went dry. 'Why, no. Nobody else.'

But just at that moment a young woman came through a door to another part of the building. 'Wes, Dad says he can't find that straw hat you got out for him.' She saw the others. 'Oh. I didn't know you had business.'

A quick look of desperation grabbed Seger's face. 'You go back there and tend to him, Effie. I'll be through here directly.'

13

'You stay put,' Guthrie told her quietly. 'And call the old man in here.'

Seger's wife was young-looking and rather attractive. Young Garrett eyed her appreciatively.

'What's this all about?' she asked tentatively.

'It's about that company safe over there,' Morgan growled out. 'You better do like that fellow tells you.'

A few minutes later they were all in the big waiting room together. Ned was a thin, stoop-shouldered man with balding hair, and Effie's elderly father was a small and white-haired fellow wearing what looked like a permanent frown. They all stared warily around the room at the intruders.

'Now, listen up, everybody,' Guthrie told them. 'Your safety may depend on it.'

He turned to Simon Tate. 'Go outside and keep a lookout.'

Tate looked disappointed. 'Sure.' A moment later he was gone, and the gunmen were reduced to four. More, Guthrie now realized, than they would need.

'All right, Seger,' Guthrie resumed. 'The safe.'

'I told you,' Seger said, his tongue clicking against his mouth. 'I just can't do that, Guthrie. It's company rules.'

The old man took a feeble step forward. 'You lowlites vamoose out of here and leave this boy alone! We don't want the likes of you stinking this place up!'

Guthrie drew the Schofield .45 and fired one loud shot. It picked the old fellow off his feet and slammed him against the wall behind him, a hole in his chest from front to back. He crumpled to the floor, leaving a crimson stain on the wall.

A piercing scream issued from Effie's throat, and she ran to where her father lay, bloody, on the floor, kneeling over him and crying. 'What the hell!' Seger said thickly.

Ned's eyes were popped wide, and he was breathing hard.

'Just a demonstration of our seriousness,' Guthrie commented drily, re-holstering the weapon. He barely glanced at the old man. 'In case you figured this was some kind of game.'

'You goddam animal!' Seger cried out.

'Does Ned know the combination?' Guthrie went on, as if nothing had happened.

'No, I swear!' Ned hurriedly interposed. 'He never let me know it! It's the rules!'

'Well then. What good are you to us?' Guthrie responded in his pleasant way. He motioned to Skin Walker, and that fellow drew a Joslyn .44 from its holster and aimed it at Ned. 'May you sleep well with your ancestors,' Walker grated out in the whispery voice.

'No, wait!' Seger yelled.

Guthrie nodded to Walker, then turned to Seger. 'Oh. Am I getting your attention now?'

'I'll open the safe! Just don't kill anybody else.'

'You play it right with us, you'll be all right,' Guthrie assured him. Seger went over to the safe and began turning a big numbered dial.

Effie left her father and rushed over to him. 'Ranchers around here depend on us to keep their money safe!' she yelled at him. 'They can't kill you, or they won't get the silver anyway! This is your Mure, your life!'

Garrett walked over and pulled her away from Seger. She struggled and he enjoyed it, grabbing at her breasts.

'Don't, Effie,' Seger gasped out. 'It's all right.'

A few minutes later the safe was open and Guthrie and Morgan were emptying it out. There were three bags of silver and a few stock certificates. Guthrie was very pleased.

'Morgan and I will take it outside,' he told Walker and Garrett. 'You two take them out back. And drag the old man out there too. We'll be waiting out front.'

'What are you going to do?' Seger was asking thickly. 'You said…'

'You'll be all right. You go on now.'

Seger swallowed hard. 'What about my wife? What about Effie?'

'You'll all be together,' Guthrie replied in an off-hand manner.

Effie shouted at him. 'You sub-human! You're lower than animals!'

Guthrie ignored her completely. Then he and Morgan joined Tate outside, and loaded the silver into saddlebags. Partway through that they heard two shots ring out from behind the building. There was a scream from the woman, then a third shot. Guthrie caught Morgan's eye and nodded his approval.

Walker and Garrett joined them a moment later, and then they were riding out.

Their first foray together had been even more than Guthrie had expected. And if things went well for Guthrie, there would be much more of the same in the very near future.

As they headed out, Morgan rode up beside Guthrie.

'Are your plans still the same for that hunter that was with the sheriff the other day?'

'Yes, and make it a priority. I don't want him in my head. And let the kid do it. He needs the experience.'

Morgan nodded. 'Consider it done.' And they both spurred their mounts to leave the depot disappearing in their dust.

TWO

In a multi-room cabin an hour's ride from the Guthrie hide-out, at the foot of the mountains south of Birney Pass, the buffalo hunter-turned-trapper O'Brien was having a leisurely breakfast with his lovely wife Sarah.

O'Brien had returned to Colorado from the Indian Territory about a year ago and brought Sarah Carter with him. They had met a while before that, on the trail south to their mutual destination, a frontier town called Fort Revenge. And during their short stay there, Sarah had so endeared herself to this wild and primitive trail man that he had broken every rule of his past character and asked her to accompany him on his return north. They had gotten wed in this very cabin shortly after their arrival, when it was just a one-room trapper's cabin – that O'Brien promptly built into a real house.

It was two days after Guthrie's violent visit to the Wells Fargo depot, and a beautiful summer morning. Sarah was at a wood stove dishing up fried eggs for them, and a moment later joined O'Brien at a crude table. She sat down awkwardly because of her eight-month pregnancy, and immediately saw his pensive mood.

'Anything wrong, O'Brien?' She seldom used terms of endearment when addressing him because she sensed they made him uncomfortable.

He glanced over at her. He was a big man, wide-shouldered and athletic-looking, and wore a rawhide tunic and trousers. The tunic was belted at the waist with a thick ammo belt but no sidearm. He had never 'carried iron'. Over forty, he was a decade older than Sarah. His slicked-back hair was shoulder length and dark, with some slight graying. He wore a thick, dark mustache but had removed a beard for Sarah.

'I was talking to Sheriff Purvis. Seems there's a gang of outlaws loose in these parts somewhere.'

Sarah swallowed a bite of her egg. 'I guess I'll never really get used to this sort of thing out here.' Before she had arrived in Fort Revenge she had been a librarian in Boston, and the West had been a big adjustment for her. She stared past him to an open window. She was a lovely woman, with dark green eyes and long dark hair.

'He wanted me to give him some help.' He shook his head. 'Can you see me pinning on a badge?'

Sarah put her fork down. 'No. I wouldn't want you to. There must be plenty of men in Birney Pass who would be happy to get such a job.'

'That's what I told him. It's some low-life named Guthrie. Wanted for murder in other states. He could cause us a lot of trouble around here.'

19

Sarah knew about trouble. After a life of afternoon teas and Sunday concerts in Boston, she had had a rude awakening in the West. Even before she got to Fort Revenge, where she expected to be a mail-order bride, she had narrowly avoided death at the hands of Pawnee because she had been hidden in high rushes when her wagon was attacked. O'Brien had found her out on the prairie alone and had reluctantly accompanied her to the Territory because he was headed there to look for new trapping grounds in what was mostly Indian country. Sarah's would-be groom turned out to be an outlaw from whom O'Brien had had to defend her, and there were other things through that.

'You don't mean for us?' she finally responded. 'The trouble?'

O'Brien met her green eyes with his sober ones. 'I can't see a man like this Guthrie taking any interest in what we have here to steal. But things happen. Until we have this baby, I might want you to go into town for a while.'

Sarah frowned. 'Oh no. Don't start treating me like a china doll now. Just because I'm pregnant. You're right, nobody is going to ride way out here hoping we have something to steal in an unobtrusive little house.'

O'Brien frowned at her. In his world he had never heard the word 'unobtrusive'. He couldn't read or write, but was fluent in five Indian languages. She intended to teach him to read after the baby was born.

When she saw his face she knew the problem. 'Oh. This out-of-the-way cabin. Sorry.' She reached over and touched his thick hand. Her affection for him knew no bounds. She could not even imagine loving any other man. From that first day on the prairie when he came along and saved her, she always felt safe with him. If he was with her, she felt no harm could befall her.

'Listen, Sarah. I think you know how much you mean to me now. It ain't the trail no more. It's you.'

She smiled a lovely smile. 'I know that.'

'I'll talk to Purvis again. And if I think it's safer for you in town, you're going to have to humor me.'

She sighed. 'Have your talk with him.'

'I'll be with you most of the time until we figure this out. This morning I'm riding out to check on a couple of traps, but they're in that little creek not far from here. I'll be back in an hour or so. I got weeding to do in the bean patch, anyway, and I wanted to look at your mare's front shoe. There's stuff to keep me busy here.'

'I'll be all right,' she assured him. 'I think this might happen sooner than the doctor thinks, though.' Touching her belly.

O'Brien gave her a smile. 'Good. We're ready.' He had finished the eggs while they spoke. Now he rose and walked to a shelf, retrieved a trail-colored Stetson, and settled it on to his head. Then he picked up a Winchester 1860 lever-action rifle from where it leaned against a wall. He never went anywhere without it. It was the great buffalo hunter Jim Elder who had commented that O'Brien could hit a buffalo in the eye at five hundred yards in a stiff crosswind. With the rifle in hand, the hunter suddenly looked dangerous.

'Remember what we talked about. You see somebody coming you don't know, slide that big bolt across the door. The windows are high and hard to get through. And no matter what they say to you, tell them to come back when I'm here. This is only till we know more about this gang.'

'I remember, O'Brien.' She knew his first name, but he had asked her never to use it because he disliked it. 'Go on out and check your traps. I'll cook up a stew for later. Bring us back some pelts.'

Outside, he walked a short distance to a small barn where they kept their two mounts and a milk cow. Nearby there was a patch of ground where there was shoulder-high corn, ripening tomatoes and beans. O'Brien glanced that way as he reached the barn. All of this domesticated life was new to him. He had spent his entire life on the trail until he met Sarah. He was still getting used to the change.

In the barn he saddled up a horse he had had just a short time. The appaloosa he had always hunted with had finally died on their way north, and he had had to acquaint himself with a new animal. It nickered now as he cinched up its saddle, and he touched its muzzle.

'Yeah. You're ready for an outing, I know. You'll like it down by the creek.' The horse nickered again, responding. It was a big dark chestnut stallion, with a white diamond on its forehead and white 'socks'.

In less than a half-hour O'Brien and the stallion were at the small gurgling creek where he had placed two traps near a beaver dam. The second trap had a large dead beaver in it, and O'Brien was pleased. With the stallion picketed thirty yards away downstream, O'Brien bent to the task of skinning his prey with the big Bowie knife he carried in a boot sheath. He would do a first scraping here, and a second at the cabin, where he would hang it out in the sun to cure the hide. He had just cut the pelt clear when his horse whinnied softly.

O'Brien turned curiously to the stallion, then got the scent. When he turned to look behind him, he saw three lean gray wolves not twenty yards away. He had missed the sound of their approach because of the gurgling stream in front of him.

'Sonofabitch,' he muttered softly. The blood-stained knife was still in his hand, but his rifle was on the horse.

The wolves were fairly large ones and looked very hungry. They had been attracted by the slaughtered beaver, but now they looked more interested in O'Brien. And his mount. They were in a wide semi-circle and had him flanked, the one on his right between him and the horse. And they had him up against the stream. He could turn and try to get across it before they caught him, but that would entail turning his back on them, and making himself very vulnerable.

They were growling quietly now, and moving closer. They meant business.

He and the horse would make several meals. And they would take him out first. O'Brien yelled at them, and waved the Bowie. They were not impressed. He faked a charge toward them, and they held their ground.

He knew there was no way he could kill all three of them with a skinning knife before they tore him up. He needed the rifle.

He made up his mind. Picking up the beaver pelt, he slowly edged his way toward the horse, which was now straining at its picket. If it broke loose and ran, it was over for him. He moved another few feet, and the wolves followed, coming closer again. The one that had been farthest to his right was very close.

Suddenly O'Brien hurled the beaver pelt at the closest wolf, and it hit the animal in the head. The wolf stopped in its tracks, shaking its head, and then was examining the pelt on the ground. The others had gathered around it. They were momentarily distracted.

O'Brien ran for his horse and was there in a moment. He grabbed at the saddle scabbard on the near side as the horse reared slightly, and slid the Winchester free as the wolves now rushed him. The rifle exploded twice in the morning quiet, and the two closest animals jerked in mid-air and fell at O'Brien's feet, hit in the chest and head. But now the third one hit O'Brien with its full weight, knocking him to the ground, its jaws trying to get at his throat. O'Brien, though, had sheathed the bloody Bowie before he made his move toward his horse, and now he drew the big blade and shoved it hard into the wolf's chest until it reached the heart.

The wolf made a sound in its throat and collapsed off him. Its legs jerked about for a moment, and it died there.

The stallion was very excited. But when it saw O'Brien was all right it settled down.

He got awkwardly to his feet. · 'It's all right now,' he told it. He patted its rump. 'Now let's get that pelt back and get out of here.'

It had been one of those unexpectedly violent outings on the trail. But he had always survived them. So far.

***

At about that same time, two men rode into view of the cabin and reined in fifty yards away from it. It was Avery Morgan and young Eben 'One Shot' Garrett, and they had been sent by Wade Guthrie to kill O'Brien.

They sat their mounts quietly in the clearing that looked toward the barn and cabin. It was a peaceful scene. Smoke drifted from a brick chimney, and the sound of a cow lowing came from the barn.

'Well. This is it,' Morgan grunted out, his heavily lined face lightly dewed with perspiration. 'This is the hunter's place. Has a nice look to it. I wouldn't have expected that.'

'Is he there? I don't see no mount anywhere.'

'It would be in the barn,' Morgan explained patiently. 'I hear he took a wife. She could be there.'

He glanced over at Garrett. 'You know what that means, don't you?'

Garrett nodded. 'I did the job at the depot, didn't I?'

'We'd better leave the mounts here. Them trail men can hear a twig breaking at a hundred yards. And I want to surprise him.'

A moment later they had dismounted and picketed their horses with picket stakes in the ground.

Inside the cabin, Sarah was cutting some carrots to go into a stew she was making for O'Brien. The big front door was closed but not bolted, and she was concentrating on what she was doing. She didn't hear the soft footsteps outside, and was surprised when she heard it open behind her. She thought it was O'Brien.

'Oh. You're back!' Then she turned and saw Morgan come through the big door, followed by Eben Garrett. Guns drawn.

Her pretty face showed shock. 'Who are you, and what are you doing in my house?' she asked breathlessly.

They were looking the place over, and noting that O'Brien was nowhere in sight. Garrett the womanizer was staring at her big belly, but she looked very good to him anyway. He came over closer to her and looked her up and down.

'Well, now.'

Big brawny Morgan ignored that. 'Where's O'Brien?'

Sarah swallowed hard. She didn't like the way Garrett was looking at her. 'He's around here somewhere. He's in and out. Did you check the tomato patch?'

Morgan's leathery face broke a small grin. 'He's not in no tomato patch, sweetheart. He's out trapping, ain't he?'

'I don't really know. He was gone before I was up.' Her heart was thumping her chest. 'Maybe you should come back at some other time.'

One Shot Garrett took hold of her arm. 'You're a real pretty one, ain't you? You his wife?' They had holstered the guns.

Sarah jerked free of him, gasping. She still held a paring knife in her right hand but didn't even know it was there. 'I want you both to leave now. O'Brien might be gone all day.'

'Now that ain't a bit friendly, honey,' Garrett purred. 'We just got here.'

He reached out and touched her dark hair, and she flinched.

'You watch her while I take a look around,' Morgan told the younger man. 'There might be something of value lying around here somewhere.'

Sarah got some courage back. 'You're going to steal from O'Brien?' she said caustically.

Morgan eyed her. 'What if I did?'

She tried to smile through her raw fear. 'I just wouldn't advise it.'

Morgan grunted. 'I'll keep taking my advice from Wade Guthrie if you don't mind, girlie.' He had

27

looked some shelves over, and now opened a door to a bedroom. 'Where do you keep your working cash?'

'We don't keep any here,' she lied.

A hard grin. 'We won't leave till we find it.'

Her mouth had gone dry. 'I should warn you. O'Brien won't like this. Not at all.'

'Ain't she a feisty little honey badger?' Garrett grinned widely.

But Morgan had disappeared into the other room. Garrett moved in very close to Sarah.

'Is that the bedroom he went to?' Sarah hesitated. 'Yes.'

'I bet you and that mountain man have yourseffs a good time in there, don't you, sweetheart?'

Sarah sucked her breath in. 'Damn you! Get out of my house!' 'Oh, we'll be gone. Eventually.'

Avery Morgan emerged from the bedroom looking nettled. 'All right, lady. I've lost my patience with you.' He drew a Remington Army .44 from its low-slung holster and held it up in front of her face, and Sarah gasped again. With all of her small adventures in the Great West, she hadn't yet had a gun in her face. 'Now, you tell us where we can find something worth carrying away with us, or I'll blow the back of that pretty head off with this.'

Sarah could hardly speak. 'In the cookie jar. Under the dry sink.'

Morgan holstered the gun. 'That's more like it.' He went to the cupboard under the sink and found the jar. It had a handful of silver coins in it.

He looked it over. 'This is everything?'

'Yes.'

Morgan stuffed it into a poke on his belt: 'Now. Where did O'Brien go trapping?'

'I honestly don't know,' she lied.

'Well, there's a small creek not far from here. We'll probably find him there. What do you think, kid? You ready to ride?'

'Not quite,' Garrett grinned, looking at Sarah.

Morgan gave him a look. 'Good God, she's pregnant, boy.'

'And ripe as a low-hanging pear,' Garrett parried. He grabbed her arm again. Now she was very scared, but did not show it to him. 'You hurt me and he'll skin you alive,' she gasped out.

'Who, the hunter? You let me worry about him.' He started to pull her to the bedroom door.

'No, wait,' Morgan interrupted gruffly. He sat down at the kitchen table. 'I see a pan of cornbread over there. Why don't you fetch that for me, missie? Before you go off to have your fun.' A dark grin.

'Oh, hell, Avery,' Garrett complained, reluctantly releasing her. Sarah pulled her arm away and rubbed at it, glad for the delay. She moved warily to a sideboard, discarding the paring knife she still held to the pocket of a small apron. She got the baking tin of cornbread and carried it to Morgan slowly, trying to think of some way to defend herself, but she knew there was none.

'Hey. This looks good. You a good cook?'

'For God's sake, Avery. That's enough.' From an impatient and heated Garrett.

'Oh, hell. Take her.' Prying out a slice of the bread.

At that same moment a short distance from the cabin, O'Brien was returning home with the beaver pelt across his saddle roll, and he was reflecting on his dramatic life change just a year ago in Fort Revenge, when he had made the world-shaking decision to take Sarah with him. O'Brien had been a loner all his adult life since his family had been taken down with the diphtheria back in the Shenandoah when he was still in his teens. He had drifted west then, trying to find a future for himself. He had driven shotgun for Wells Fargo, lived with a tribe of Lakota Sioux for a while, and then worked for a big hide company where he learned about buffalo hunting.

Later he had gone off on his own, or sometimes partnered up with another hunter, such as Shanghai Smith or Jim Elder. He had spent his life on the trail, almost never sleeping in a hotel bed, and avoiding towns entirely unless he needed ammo or provisions. They had been hard scrabble days, stalking big herds, 'busting every rise on your belly like a goddam snake', roasting a buffalo steak on a mesquite stick, with corn dodgers and chicory coffee, in hardship camp. But he had loved every minute of it. On one hunt he had had to cut the belly of a 'shaggy' open, gut it, and climb inside to avoid being burned alive by a prairie fire. He and Shanghai had both come close to death in buffalo stampedes and other mishaps.

That had all ended, though, before he left Colorado for the Territory. In recent years the big herds had disappeared because of over-hunting by the hide companies, and it had been more trapping for him than hunting. And then came Sarah. The first woman he had ever had the time even to take notice of since his mother and sister.

He was a hundred yards from the cabin now, and pulled the stallion to a halt. He had seen the two mounts picketed on the slope leading to the cabin. 'What the hell,' he muttered.

He dismounted beside the other horses, and they shied away for a moment, but settled down when he let the stallion greet them. He studied the cabin and saw that the door stood open. It had been closed when he left.

He deftly removed a spur from his stove-pipe boot, and then the other. He slid the Winchester rifle from its saddle scabbard and headed for the cabin on foot.

Inside, Garrett had just grabbed Sarah's arm again, but she had successfully torn free of him, breathing hard.

'You scum! You'll be very sorry for this!' Her eyes were moist now, and her cheeks were flushed.

Morgan rose from the table. 'I'm heading back to the mounts. You can catch up with me.'

Garrett didn't respond. He was feeling too much heat for Sarah now. 'You might as well go peaceful, honey. It will be more fun for you.'

He grabbed both arms then, and brushed a breast. Sarah remembered the paring knife, and slid it from the apron pocket. Breaking that arm free for a moment, she brought it across Garrett's face.

31

The blade made a shallow cut across Garrett's left cheek, and took him by surprise. 'Hey!' he yelled out. He released her arm and she stepped back two steps.

Garrett was furious. 'Well, that's it, you little bitch.' He drew the deadly Tranter .38 at his hip and levelled it at her chest.

'Put one in her and let's get out of here,' Morgan said curtly. 'We have more important things to...'

They both turned at a slight sound behind them, and saw O'Brien in the doorway. He filled its entrance like a grizzly.

Nobody said a word.

One Shot Garrett's gun was already out, and he turned it now on O'Brien, with an air of supreme confidence.

But before he could squeeze the trigger on the Tranter, the Winchester roared in the room, the hot lead punching Garrett just over the heart, and throwing him violently across the kitchen table, not far from Sarah. He hit the floor behind it, taking the table with him.

Morgan had drawn his Remington Army while that was happening, and now quickly fired off a shot at O'Brien's chest. But O'Brien had levered the big rifle and re-aimed immediately after firing at Garrett, and had ducked into a low crouch. Morgan's shot tore at O'Brien's tunic at the shoulder, hitting only rawhide, and then a second explosion from the rifle struck Morgan just above his nose, traveled through his brain pan like a hot poker, and blew off the back of his skull. He went running backwards until he smashed hard into a wall behind him, where he slowly collapsed to the floor, a blue hole in his forehead.

Gunsmoke was thick in Sarah's nostrils as she stood there wide-eyed from the action. She had never seen anything like this from him.

He came on into the room, frowning. He hadn't even taken a second look at the corpses on the floor. He and Sarah met at the center of it, and she fell into his arms.

'Are you all right?'

She wiped at a tear and gave him a tired but lovely smile. 'I am now.' He nodded. He turned from her, went and leaned the rifle on a wall, and stepped over Garrett's body to get to the stove. 'I need a hot cup. I been thirsty all morning. I'll clean all this up directly.'

Sarah watched him with a smug smile on her pretty face. He didn't tell her about the wolves. And he never would.

THREE

Within a half-hour of the cabin shoot-out O'Brien had dragged the bodies of Morgan and Garrett outside and straightened up the room it had happened in. Sarah had calmed down from her ugly encounter with them, and continued preparing O'Brien's midday meal, while O'Brien brought all three horses up to the cabin and hitched them to a short hitching rail there. Not long after he had cleaned up and was ready to eat, hoping Sarah didn't notice the scratch on his neck from the wolf that got to him. The stew she had made him was ready, and he ate it hungrily. Sarah ate more slowly, watching him eat, just enjoying his presence.

'Did they say who they were?' he finally asked her when his plate was almost empty.

It always amazed her to see how physical violence seemed such an ordinary thing to him. She was surprised he was even talking about it.

'One of them mentioned Wade Guthrie. Isn't that the outlaw the sheriff was discussing with you?'

He nodded, frowning.

'They came after you, O'Brien. They were going to kill you.' He gave her a half-smile. 'I ain't that easy to kill.'

She returned the smile. 'I tried to tell them.'

His face went sober. 'Why would this pond scum want to bother with me?'

'He might have seen you talking to Purvis and thought you would be a danger to him if he was working this area.'

'He sounds smarter than most of them.' He put his fork down. 'Look, I have to take them bodies in to Purvis. Talk this over with him. And I'm taking you with me. You ain't safe out here alone no more.'

'Nobody will come here again until Guthrie finds out what happened.' He caught her gaze in an iron-hard one. 'I ain't arguing this, Sarah. You don't have no vote in a thing like this.'·

She sighed, and nodded. 'I understand.'

'We'll leave as soon as you clean this up. I'll get your sorrel mare ready for you.'

Not long after that they were riding out, with the two bodies slung over the saddles of their mounts.

It was a two-hour ride to Birney Pass. When O'Brien had been trapping in the area before he went south, it had had a crooked city marshal who had tried to steal O'Brien's pelts one spring day, and had paid the ultimate price, for which the little town was grateful. Since then the county seat had been moved to Birney Pass, and Sheriff Purvis had established his office and jail there.

O'Brien and Sarah rode down a long, dusty street with houses, a saloon, a general store and a boarding house. At the far end was a building with a sign out front that announced simply SHERIFF. They reined in there and Sarah sat her mount while O'Brien checked inside. Riding was hard for Sarah in these last weeks, and she tiredly held her swollen belly now. Inside, O'Brien was told by a young, acne-faced deputy that Purvis was at home. So O'Brien led Sarah the few blocks to Purvis' house, trailing the outlaws behind them.

As they dismounted, Purvis emerged from the front door to greet them. 'O'Brien! And you brought your beautiful wife. What a pleasure for us!'

'Sheriff,' Sarah greeted him with a smile.

'Say, what's this you brought me?' Purvis wondered, staring at the two bodies draped over their horses.

'Just a couple of no-goods that come to our place with bad intentions,' O'Brien said casually.

'Not a good idea,' Sarah said proudly.

Purvis gave a little laugh. 'I see what you mean. Who are they, do you know?'

'They're Guthrie's men,' O'Brien told him. 'He's taken a disliking to me, I reckon. It won't be the first time.'

'Hmm. I wonder if he saw you palavering with me the other day.' Confirming what Sarah had guessed.

'Well, these two are yours now,' O'Brien responded.

Purvis nodded. 'I'll take them around back till the mortician can pick them up. You two come on in and we'll talk this over.'

When they all entered the house, the sheriff's wife Dru was in the wide parlor to meet them. She had met Sarah just once before.

She came and embraced her tenderly. 'My lord, just look at you, darling!'

'It's nice to see you again, Dru. I miss female company out there sometimes.'

'Well, the Lord knows me and the sheriff would like to see more of you, Sarah. You'll have to plan more trips in for groceries and such. Ethan won't take me nowhere because he's so busy.' She was several years older than Sarah, a rather pretty woman with blonde hair going gray.

'You know that ain't my fault, Missus,' Purvis defended himself. 'Especially now. With Guthrie in the neighborhood.' He had just heard of the depot hold-up. 'Set down, folks. You had a long ride here.' He was about O'Brien's age, a tall, slim man with an angular, weathered face and an easy smile.

O'Brien and Sarah seated themselves on a long sofa and the Purvises took soft chairs facing them. It was a well-appointed room, with an oak sideboard on one wall, and a roll-top desk on another. An oriental carpet covered the floor between the sofa and the chairs. Sarah was reminded of an even more formal home from her early days in Boston:

'Now,' Purvis said, leaning forward and clasping his hands before him. 'How much trouble did these men cause you out there?'

'I wasn't there when they come,' O'Brien told him. He grinned a rare grin. 'But Sarah handled them.'

Sarah sighed. 'I stalled them. They came there to kill O'Brien, Ethan.'

Purvis nodded. 'They might think I deputized him. A Wells Fargo depot was just robbed, and everybody there murdered. We know it was Guthrie, because a kid from a ranch saw them riding away from there, and described them. And they'll probably keep this up till somebody stops them. We have no idea where they're holed up. But it has to be somewhere in the county, I'd reckon. That puts it on me, and that kid deputy of mine who'd forget to tie his own shoelaces if somebody didn't remind him.'

'Sorry about that, Ethan,' O'Brien said quietly. 'Listen. I can't leave Sarah out at that cabin alone until this is all settled. I'm hoping I can situate her in town here for a while. Is that boarding house affordable?'

But Sarah turned to him quickly. This was her first knowledge of this idea. 'Now just a minute. You didn't discuss this with me.'

'I thought if I waited till I got to town, you'd give me less trouble,' he admitted to her.

She looked away from him. 'I'd have to think about that.'

But Dru Purvis intervened. 'Sarah, love. O'Brien is right. You can't be out there by yourself when he's gone. And you're not going to no boarding house. I'd love to have you right here. We have an extra bed here on the first floor, no climbing stairs for you. And I have the perfect person to get you through what's coming. My widow friend Olivia is a midwife, and she won't even charge you. We'll take real good care of you.'

Sarah tried a smile. 'You make it sound pretty inviting.'

'Good!' Purvis said loudly. 'Then it's settled. You're our guest till further notice! O'Brien can bring some things in from the cabin for you.'

'They're already in my saddle roll,' O'Brien said, eyeing Sarah sidewise. Sarah gave him a look.

'All right, everybody. I guess I'm out-voted.' Dru rose. 'Come on, honey. I'll show you the room.'

Sarah got up awkwardly because of her belly, and followed Dru into an adjacent room.

'I'm much obliged,' O'Brien said when they were gone.

'She'll pretty this place up a bit,' Purvis said. 'She suits Dru right down to the ground.' He leaned back on his chair. 'O'Brien, I'm going to need some help for a while because of Guthrie.'

'You can't count on the boy I met earlier?'

'I wouldn't even take him out on something like this. It would be like taking a twelve-year-old kid. I'd just get him killed.'

'I'm sorry to hear that.'

Purvis looked past O'Brien. 'They murdered everybody at the depot,' he said quietly. 'Everybody. Including the agent's wife.'

O'Brien sighed. 'Then they would have killed Sarah.'

'I'm sure of it.'

'That's the way I had it figured,' O'Brien said.

'These men are the worst we've ever seen around here. And I don't even know their whereabouts. I'll have to scrounge up a posse. People I don't know and can't depend on. I'd rather have you.'

O'Brien frowned heavily. 'Me? Wear a badge? Carry iron? Sorry, Ethan. That ain't going to happen.'

'It would be temporary.'

O'Brien shook his head. 'I'm a trapper, Ethan. A hunter. Not a lawman. I take trouble as it comes at me. I don't go looking for it. Anyway, I got traps set out there that need looking after. I got corn and beans. I'm domesticated now.' He gave a small smile. 'But mostly, when Guthrie finds out I killed two of his men, what do you think he'll do?'

'He'll come after you again.'

O'Brien nodded. 'And when he does, I want to be there.'

'I see what you mean.'

'I'll be more help to you out there than I would here.'

'You might be right. But you'd have to face them alone.'

'I'll take whatever comes at me,' O'Brien told him.

'I don't like that very much. But I guess I wouldn't bet against you.' Just then Sarah and Dru returned to the room.

'It's nice,' she told O'Brien. 'You may have trouble getting me home again.'

'I think you'll be very comfortable, Sarah,' Dru said. 'And I have a couple of great recipes for expecting women.'

'We'll buy groceries, of course,' Sarah responded.

'Don't you worry your pretty head about that,' Dru said. 'Now. Are you men ready to eat?'

Dru served the four of them chops and potatoes, and they ate at a round table in a pleasant dining room. As they ate, Dru wanted to know more about Sarah.

'You never told me how you two came together,' she said as they ate. 'Was that down in Fort Revenge?'

'Oh, no,' Sarah said. 'I was on my way south on a freight wagon that was attacked by Pawnee while I was down at a stream freshening up. The Indians never saw me, but they killed both my drivers and stole the horses. I sat there on the buckboard of that wagon all night thinking the Indians might be back at any minute. O'Brien found me out there the next morning, and he took me on down to Fort Revenge where he was headed to see an old hunting partner, Shanghai Smith.'

'Me and him had some times out on the trail,' O'Brien offered. 'We both ought to have been killed out there fifty times over. He was running a stage line down there. Told me there was good trapping for me around them parts. But it wasn't what he thought.'

'Why were you headed for the Territory?' Dru asked Sarah.

Sarah was embarrassed. 'I went as a mail-order bride. It didn't work out.' It was obvious she didn't want to talk about it.

'Sarah liked it there,' O'Brien put in. 'It was me wanted to get back to the mountains.'

'He was born for this,' Sarah said quietly.

Purvis forked up a bite of meat and spoke through it. 'I got as far south as Kansas City once. Had a bank account there. Them bankers hold on to their money like horse glue to leather.'

Sarah smiled at that. She was beginning to like both of the Purvises. She turned to O'Brien. 'So you're riding back to the cabin later?'

O'Brien nodded, giving her an affectionate look. 'I'll be in regular to see you. Make sure you're doing all right.'

'We'll let you know when she's close,' Dru said.

'You expect them to come back, don't you?' Sarah said bluntly. A heavy silence fell over the table like a night fog.

O'Brien didn't look at her. 'They might.'

Sarah looked distraught. 'Then why are you going back out there?' Now he looked at her. 'I can't quit living because of these men, Sarah. I have traps out there that need working. That's the way I make us a living. And prices are up now at Fort Griffin. And our crops have to be tended to, kind of regular. There's nobody else to do that, Sarah. It's me.'

'I'd a thousand times rather lose all of that than you,' she said, looking down at her plate.

Dru reached out and touched her arm. 'Ethan will go out there and check on him. Won't you, Sheriff?'

'Of course,' Purvis assured her. 'I can ride back out there with you when you leave and stay a few days. Before I go looking for Guthrie.'

O'Brien gave him a look. 'You know how important it is that you get right on this, Purvis.'

Another long silence, then Sarah spoke again. 'Never mind, you two. I understand the situation.'

42

She turned to O'Brien soberly. 'You go do what you have to do.' And then, acidly, 'Whatever made me think I could stop you?'

And that was the end of that conversation. Nobody thought any more needed to be said.

A couple of hours later O'Brien rode out, with Sarah watching him until he was out of sight.

***

At Wade Guthrie's primitive cabin hide-out, he and the muscular-looking half-breed Skin Walker had just finished a light midday meal and were sitting at the crude table with their empty tin plates still there. Walker was cleaning a front tooth with a pocket knife, and Guthrie was staring at an opposite wall, in deep thought. He was wondering why Morgan and Garrett hadn't returned from the hunter's cabin by now. Earlier in the day he had taken his mind off it by reading some obscure poet. He owned almost a dozen books, which he never shared with anybody, and which his current cohorts regarded with ill-concealed disdain. When he had been in the Texas Rangers, he had actually frequented a library now and then, much to the bewilderment of his comrades. Despite his sociopathic tendencies, and his utter disregard for the feelings of others, his mental acuity was superior to most, and he considered himself on a higher plane than almost anybody he met. Anybody who rode with him had to think of himself as a lowly employee not capable of serious thought.

43

'I wonder what happened to Morgan and the kid?' he finally voiced his thoughts.

'Maybe the hunter wasn't there,' Walker suggested. 'Maybe they had to wait for him.'

'If you don't put that knife down, I'm going to blow it out through the back of your thick head,' Guthrie said without emotion.

Walker laid the knife down. 'Maybe they went to town for a drink.' He wasn't easily intimidated.

'Maybe they rode off to Boulder,' Guthrie said with sarcasm. 'Why the hell should we speculate?'

'Huh?'

'Never mind. Tate rode off this morning without saying anything to me. I don't like that. Where did he go?'

'I think he mentioned riding into town.'

'He does that again, and he's out,' Guthrie said irritably. 'I want him here when the other two get back.'

'I prayed for them last night.' Guthrie frowned.

'What?'

'I prayed for Morgan and Garrett. For their success against the Created One.'

'Who? The hunter?'

'I also killed the honey badger. It has powerful medicine. It is done together with the praying.'

'In the first place, those gods you pray to don't exist. And also, if they did, they wouldn't give a rat's liver what you want. And last of all, they wouldn't pay any attention to a killer like you. Your prayers would sound false to them. Did you ever hear this? "My words fly up, my thoughts remain below; words without thoughts never to heaven go."'

'Is that from that fellow Mark Twain?' Walker wondered. 'If I could read, I'd try something by him.'

Guthrie sighed. 'Clean up the damn table, Walker. I'm tired of looking at this mess.'

But in the next moment the door opened and Simon Tate walked in. The small, blocky man came bow-legged over to them, removing a crumpled hat and wiping at his forehead with it.

'It got hot out there. My mount is lathered up.' He heaved himself on to a chair at the table near Walker.

'Where the hell have you been all this time?' Guthrie scowled at him. Tate shrugged heavy shoulders. 'I felt like getting out this morning. I rode into Birney Pass.'

'I told you,' Walker reminded Guthrie.

Guthrie ignored him. 'We don't need provisions. And you left without permission.'

'Permission? Hell, Wade. I needed a drink. I spent a little time at that pigsty of a saloon there.'

'Maybe I didn't make myself clear,' Guthrie said evenly. 'You check with me when you leave here, while we're holed up here together. Do it again, and you'll be gone.'

The small man's flat, wizened face grew belligerent. He was known to have a quick and often unreasonable temper. 'You're threatening to fire me because I needed a drink? I never had to ask no permission to get myself a Planter's Rye before. Goddam it, keep a supply here!'

'There will be no alcohol in this cabin while we're in the middle of this little campaign of ours. This is serious stuff. In case you hadn't figured that out.'

Tate's face changed, and a look of satisfaction came over it. He had just remembered something he had heard in town. Tate was not only quick-tempered but rather dense. 'Maybe you'll be glad I went when you hear the news.'

Guthrie frowned. 'News? What news?'

Tate looked smug. 'I was talking to this boy that knows Purvis. He had just spoken to him when he saw Purvis on the way from his house to the jail. It seems Purvis had just sent a couple of bodies over to the mortician.'

'Yes?' Guthrie said impatiently.

'Well, you know. I thought of Morgan and Garrett right away.'

Guthrie's face revealed several emotions flitting through him simultaneously. 'Why the hell would you think it was them? It could have been anybody.'

'Well, the thing is this. Just before this fellow spoke to the sheriff, he saw a man riding out of town wearing rawhides.'

Walker turned his face to the ceiling, closed his eyes, and muttered something in Lakota.

Guthrie had developed a fierce look on his broken-nose face, and was directing it at Tate. 'You goddam low-grade moron! You knew all that when you walked in here, and just now decided to tell us?'

46

Tate's broad face colored slightly. 'Nobody calls me a moron!'

Walker had focused on Guthrie. 'O'Brien killed them,' he said. 'Both of them. Makes you think.'

Guthrie rose from his chair, and began pacing the room. 'That isn't possible. They were both top guns. And the hunter doesn't even carry iron. There must be some mistake.'

Tate had cooled down some. With a sullen look, he grunted out, 'He could have heard it wrong. Or maybe I did. I'm a moron, remember?'

Guthrie ignored him as if he hadn't spoken.

'You heard it right,' Walker put in quietly. 'I've had a bad feeling about this since they left this morning. I guess you were right about the prayers, Wade. Or maybe I didn't gut that badger the right way.'

'Will you shut up about the goddam badger!' Guthrie yelled at Walker. 'My God! Both Morgan and Garrett gone, and look what I'm left with!'

He threw himself onto the straight chair he had vacated, and hung his head over the table. 'I've known Avery for a decade. He's the only one of you misfits I could really rely on.'

They watched him silently. It was best not to say anything when he was in this kind of mood. He might just draw that Schofield .45 and casually put a chunk of hot lead through your right eyeball.

'Well. I can't go for stage coaches and banks with the likes of you two. And your story must be right, since they haven't showed back here. Sonofabitch.' More silence.

47

Guthrie looked over at Walker. 'Say, didn't you tell me you'd seen Brett St Clair in a saloon over in Scottville a few weeks ago?'

Walker nodded. 'He was dealing One-Eyed Jacks at a faro table. I don't really know him, so I didn't speak.'

Guthrie absorbed that. 'Brett did a couple of jobs with me when I first got out of the Rangers. He's got a head on his shoulders. I think we might ride over there tomorrow. See if he's interested in our big plans.'

'Can he shoot?' Tate asked sourly.

'He would make you look a little awkward,' Guthrie retorted.

'I can shoot,' Tate said. 'If I'd been with Morgan and Garrett, the hunter would be dead.'

'If you'd been there,' Walker said acidly, 'you'd be dead.'

That got Guthrie to thinking about O'Brien again. 'Well, tomorrow we'll go find St Clair. Then, before we do our next job, I have a little payback planned for that hunter. This time we'll go there in force. And we won't leave till his blood is decorating that cabin of his.'

Tate was relaxed again. 'And you'll see what this gun can do,' he responded darkly.

FOUR

O'Brien checked the cabin over carefully on his return from Birney Pass. And he hadn't been there over a half-hour before he began missing Sarah. There were two things in his life important to him now: being out there on the trail hunting and trapping, and Sarah. And Sarah now assumed priority over everything else.

The cabin was just as they had left it. Guthrie hadn't paid a second visit. The following morning O'Brien decided to make an overnight trip out, to set some traps on a couple of creeks several hours ride from the cabin. He had heard there were beaver in big numbers farther south, and maybe even ermine, which brought a lot more on the Fort Garland market.

At the end of the cabin structure O'Brien had built a small utility room for provisions and equipment. Before he rode out he went in there and found four iron traps and some ammo. As a last thought, and for no logical reason, he grabbed the big Sharps .500 buffalo gun that lately he had left at home. Since he was making a foray away from his usual grounds, he figured anything could happen.

He closed up the cabin and rode out. It was a long ride, and he didn't arrive at the first creek until mid-afternoon. He spent some more time finding a big beaver dam and setting two traps near it. Then, in early evening, he found the second stream with evidence of ermine nearby, and set the other two traps.

He had had a big day. He found a shady spot under a close-by cottonwood, and made hardship camp there, building a fire and making himself a meal of salt pork, a tomato from his garden, a Sarah-made biscuit, and real coffee. It was luxury in comparison to the old days with Shanghai.

He was just cleaning up after his meal, at dark, when he heard a rider approaching his camp.

O'Brien had been preoccupied with his work, and hadn't heard the intruder until he was just outside camp. His long guns were still on the stallion's irons. His only weapon was the Bowie skinning knife in his boot scabbard. He swore under his breath. He always liked to be well prepared for unexpected visitations on the trail.

The stranger rode up into the light of the camp.

O'Brien looked him over, wondering if he should make a move toward his guns. But the stranger looked rather harmless. He was armed, but he was a dumpy-looking man with a belly, and the weapon on his hip looked like an old out-of-date Colt.

He tipped his hat. 'Evening, mister. No need for alarm. I'm just a down-on-my-luck drummer hoping you got a cup of coffee you can spare a tired traveler.'

It was an unwritten law of the trail to accede to such a request, and O'Brien had never denied a cup to a respectable-looking stranger.

O'Brien sighed audibly. 'Hell, why not?' he said curtly. 'The pot is still hot.' 'Much obliged,' the big-belly stranger grinned. He dismounted clumsily and came up by the fire. He had rheumy eyes, and ears that stuck out sideways. 'I could've drunk swamp water.'

O'Brien poured him a cup of coffee and watched him gulp some down. 'My name is Davis,' the other man announced. 'Ben Davis. I just rode over from Billings. That's come to be a wide open town. You ever been there?'

O'Brien ignored the question.

'You run into any shaggies over that way?'

'Buffalo? Oh, no. They're all cleaned out around there. There was a big hide company near there, you know; for a while the bone wagons would pass through town loaded to overflowing. The prairie was littered with them.'

O'Brien shook his head. 'That's what I figured.'

Davis sat down on a stump near the fire without being invited. 'You done much buff hunting, mister?'

O'Brien let him sit. 'I done my share.'

'Say, might I ask your name?'

Before O'Brien could answer a coyote howled into the night nearby, and Davis looked out there warily.

51

'The name's O'Brien. That coyote won't come into camp.'

'I used to use them for target practice,' Davis said soberly, 'when I was better with this thing.' He indicated the old Colt.

O'Brien wished he hadn't let him sit. Any coyote was more valuable to the world than men like Davis.

'I notice you don't carry,' Davis then said casually.

'A sidearm don't make much of an impression on a buff weighing almost a ton,' O'Brien commented. 'I never had no use for one.'

Davis nodded. 'I see what you mean. Say, you carry any cash in them saddlebags? For ammo and such, you know. If you ain't armed, somebody could come along and take that from you.'

O'Brien turned a brittle stare on him. 'And why would that interest you?' Davis looked sheepish. He reached to his belt and drew the old Colt.

'You don't know how embarrassing this is for me. After you giving me coffee and all. But I'm stony lonesome desperate, I got to admit. I'm going to have to have whatever you got in them bags.'

O'Brien regarded him with open surprise. 'Are you serious?'

'Oh, yes, sir.'

O'Brien sighed again. 'A man tried to steal my pelts at the Fort Griffin Rendezvous once. I took a gun away from him that looked a lot like yours, and fractured his jaw in three places.'

Davis swallowed his sudden tension. He had stood up now.

'Wait a minute. Did you call yourself O'Brien?'

'You heard it right,' the hunter told him.

'O'Brien. The Fort Griffin Rendezvous. My God. You're that White Lakota, ain't you?'

'Is that important to you, you goddam coffee thief?'

Davis re-holstered the Colt so quickly it almost fell to the ground. 'Jesus and Mary! Forget I said anything!' Breathlessly. 'I don't know what got into me! I didn't know!'

O'Brien was shaking his head. He walked to his horse and pulled a bag of back-up chicory from a saddlebag, and threw it into Davis's hands. 'Here. This will give you something to drink for a few days. Now get the hell out of here while I'm still in a good mood.'

Davis couldn't believe it. 'Damn!' He looked at the bag, then up at O'Brien. 'You'd do this after....'

'Get on your horse and make tracks,' O'Brien growled at him, becoming impatient.

'I'm already gone,' Davis assured him. And a moment later, he was.

***

In Birney Pass, Sarah was settling in comfortably. She was helping Dru with cooking, and surprised her hostess with her skill at it. The next morning after her arrival, when O'Brien was still out on the trail, Purvis had had an early breakfast by himself and had left for his office down the street. Sarah and Dru sat at the kitchen table then, and had a more leisurely meal. Sarah was still eating well, and she thought that was a good sign for her pregnancy. She had asked the local doctor to see her later, and he was coming to the house to examine her.

'You look like he's ready to bust out of there,' Dru told her as they sat finishing their coffee. She gave a small laugh. She and Sarah had guessed that because of her size, and all the kicking in there, that it had to be a boy, and Sarah knew that would please O'Brien.

'I feel like it could happen any minute,' Sarah said. 'I'll be glad to get the doctor's ideas about it.'

'He's a good doc,' Dru assured her. 'He tends to Ethan and me whenever we need him. He even brought my Luke into the world. He's gone now, out in Wyoming Territory somewhere. Droving cattle. Say, I'm going to walk down to Olivia Avery's place while you're seeing the doctor. Arrange for her to be here when it happens. She's brought dozens of squalling youngsters into the big world. You'll be glad to have her.'

'I'm sure of it, and thanks,' Sarah smiled at her.

Dru sat back on her chair. 'I've been thinking on this, dear. How did you ever get that wild man to bring you north with him? He doesn't seem the type to settle down with a woman.' She gave a sour smile. 'I tell you, if Ethan didn't already know him, I'd be scared of him.'

Sarah offered her a sympathetic look. 'Oh, Dru. He's perfectly harmless. He treats me like I'm the Queen of Sheba. You should see him in one of his tender moments.'

Dru gave her a look. 'I wouldn't think him capable of a tender moment. Oh, I shouldn't have said that, honey. Me and my big mouth.'

'No, it's all right,' Sarah told her. 'I've seen women cross the street when they see him coming. And an occasional man. I think it's his manner.'

'It's not his manner,' Dru countered. 'It's his physical presence. And those eyes. They look right through you.'

Sarah didn't take offense. 'I hope you get to know him better. You'll get to like him. And if he likes you, he'll lay his life down for you.'

'It sounds like you like him just a little bit.'

Sarah gave a small sigh. 'I've never felt anything like this for a man. I wouldn't want to go on without him.'

'Oh, dear. You do have it bad.'

'Isn't that the way it's supposed to be?' Sarah suggested.

'Well. He got himself a Sears Roebuck doll when he run on to you, Sarah darling. I hope he knows how lucky he is.'

Sarah looked past her. 'On that whole ride to the Territory he barely took notice of me. As a woman, I mean. He hardly knew how to talk to me, or act around me. Women were never a part of his life. But down there that slowly changed.'

'Any other man would have jumped on you at first sight,' Dru laughed. 'Well, at least it all turned out fine. How does he feel about the baby?'

'I think it scared him at first,' Sarah admitted. 'But now I think he's as excited as I am about it. He feels my belly almost every day.'

Dru looked sober. 'I'm real sorry you two got mixed up in Ethan's problems. I really am. I'd hate it if something happened to that hunter of yours. But of course we'd take care of you, I want you to know that, Sarah.'

That made Sarah's eyes tear up a little. 'That's very nice, Dru. But O'Brien has been through this sort of thing before. I think he'll find a way to handle it.'

Dru thought to herself that he might not have had to deal with a man as ruthless as Guthrie. But she didn't voice it. 'I'm sure everything will work out just fine,' she offered.

She had just finished speaking those words when a knocking came at the front door, and it was the doctor. Dru let him in, and he came and introduced himself to Sarah. He was a small man with spectacles and a short mustache. He carried a black medical kit bag.

'Well. What a lovely patient,' he smiled at her. 'Why haven't you been around to see me sooner, young lady? You look very far advanced.'

'I live quite a distance from town,' Sarah explained. 'But everything seems all right.'

The doctor arranged with Dru to take Sarah into her bedroom then, and he proceeded to examine her there, as she lay on the bed. Sarah's dress came off, and most of her undergarments, and then she was exposing her belly to him. He felt about carefully, over and over, and then put a stethoscope on it. Finally, he spoke to her.

'What is your age, young lady?'

Sarah told him she was just over thirty, and waited for his reaction. 'And you haven't given birth before?'

She shook her pretty head.

'Well. You're within a week or so of delivery. But your baby seems a bit mis-positioned in there. It could cause you some trouble when it happens. And at your age, that could be somewhat risky for you.'

Sarah looked past him to the ceiling. 'How much risk?'

He shrugged. 'It's hard to say until the moment. But with a little luck you'll be all right.'

Sarah thought of O'Brien, and everything he already had on his mind. 'Can we keep this just between us, Doctor? I think it would be better for all concerned.'

'Of course, Sarah. But I understand you're bringing Olivia Avery in to help. She ought to know.'

Sarah nodded in agreement. 'I'll tell her when it's necessary.'

'Fine. Listen, if you need me before the big event, just tell Dru to come and get me.'

'I'll do that,' Sarah told him.

A half-hour after he was gone, and Sarah was dressed again, Dru returned from her visit to Olivia Avery. Sarah was having a cup of coffee in the kitchen.

'Olivia will be glad to help us through this,' she announced. 'And she won't take a fee. She might drop past tomorrow to take a look at you. How did it go with the doc?'

'Oh, he agreed I'm very close,' Sarah replied evasively. 'He was glad we're getting help.'

'Is everything all right down there?'

Sarah hesitated. 'He thinks I'll be okay.'

'That husband of yours better get back to town or he'll miss the whole show!' Dru smiled.

'I know he hates it that he's not here,' Sarah sighed. 'But even when he's out there he's a right to know what's happening here now, Dru.'

'Well, Ethan can ride out for him as soon as you think you're close.'

'Yes,' Sarah responded. 'That's just what we'll do.'

Dru studied her face. 'You'll be glad when this is all over, won't you, dear?'

Sarah gave her a dour look. 'You have no idea,' she said quietly.

***

Later that same morning O'Brien was down at the further creek to check on his traps there, and found that he had had no luck so far. He would now ride back to the beaver traps and check them out before returning to the cabin, which was a long ride. Whatever the result there, he would check on the traps in the stream nearest the cabin on his way back.

It was a beautiful Colorado morning. The sun had risen in golden splendor, streaking the eastern sky with ribbons of crimson as it climbed into a lofty dome of light blue. To the west were snow peaks despite the summer weather, and between him and them were expanses of shoulder-high grass dotted with aspens and cottonwoods. It all reminded O'Brien why he loved living out on the trail, away from civilization and the complexity of human society.

He was just preparing to head back north to the other stream when he heard a rider coming up from the south. He muttered something under his breath. Davis, and now this. What he wanted out there was to be completely alone. He had no interest in wasting his time palavering with some boring traveler. He cinched a saddle strap up as the stranger approached. When the rider was within a few yards, he looked up sourly, then took a second look.

The rider, a short, dumpy-looking man who resembled Davis, was staring hard at O'Brien.

'Oh, my God!'

O'Brien could hardly believe his eyes: it was R.C. Funk, one of Shanghai Smith's stagecoach drivers from Fort Revenge. Over a thousand miles away, in the Indian Territory.

'O'Brien?' Funk called out.

O'Brien let a rare smile edge its way on to his very masculine, trail-weathered face. 'The same, Funk. What the hell are you doing, clear up here? I thought I'd never see the likes of you again.'

'I'm on my way to Montana. Got a cousin over there that wants me to help him run a ranch. I thought I'd give it a try. I thought if I came this way, I'd find your cabin and say hello to you and that good-looking woman of yours, and jaw about old times at the Territorial Express.'

He dismounted, and came over to O'Brien and hugged him before O'Brien could stop him.

'All right, all right,' O'Brien said testily. He looked him over. 'You gained a little more weight, boy.'

'That will come off at the ranch,' Funk said breezily. 'You look exactly the same, partner. Like you could wrestle steers. How's Sarah?'

'Getting ready to give me a son,' O'Brien said.

'Oh, my Lord! Congratulations! She always looked fertile, if you know what I mean. No offense.'

O'Brien sighed. 'None taken. So what's happening down there in the Territory? Is the Express making any money?'

'Oh, yes. They're still running the same lines. Old Scratch is still driving, and Cinch Bug. They ain't got no shotgun rider now. That all changed when the new owners took over.'

O'Brien frowned. 'New owners?'

Funk screwed his face up. 'Oh... I thought you knew.' Then his face changed. 'Oh, Jesus. You don't know.'

'I don't get no news out here,' O'Brien said curiously.

'Well... Shanghai Smith is dead.' He watched O'Brien's face.

O'Brien felt a weight grab on to his midsection and try to pull him to the ground. 'Dead? Smitty dead?'

'We think it was his heart. Hell, I'm sorry, O'Brien. I thought you knew.'

O'Brien felt a little light-headed. He turned and walked to a nearby stump and sat down on it. After

Sarah, Smith had been the most important person in O'Brien's life. Their time together went back two decades.

'Sonofabitch,' he finally mumbled.

'He went fast,' Funk was saying. 'He might not even have known it was happening.'

O'Brien nodded absently. 'He ought to have died years ago. The life he led. Just like me.'

'I'm real sorry.'

'It's all right, Funk. I'll get over it. In time. Smitty was one of the big names. Him and Jim Elder and a couple others.'

'And you,' Funk said.

O'Brien rose heavily from the stump. He could not tell Sarah until after her delivery. She loved Smitty. 'Well, I'd like to invite you to the cabin, but I got some trapping to do. And Sarah ain't there. So I guess I'll have to say my goodbyes here. It was good seeing you again, though. It put Fort Revenge right back in my head again.'

Funk nodded. 'Wish I hadn't had to bring you bad news.' He prepared to mount up again. 'Oh. I hear there's some bad people terrorizing your area around here. And they're out recruiting. Better be careful for a while.'

O'Brien frowned. 'Yes, I will be.' Guthrie was responding to the attrition. Like a smart general. 'Be careful out there yourself.'

Funk was mounted again. 'I will.' He looked thoughtful for a moment. 'Say, talking about buffalo, I just come across a small herd late last night.

Chewing their cuds into a westerly wind about an hour's ride south of here. In a green valley. In case you're interested.'

O'Brien was pulled out of his thoughts. 'What? You saw buffalo?'

'Absolutely. You'll recognize the site. It's near a small stream.'

O'Brien couldn't believe it. He hadn't seen a herd of buff since heading down to the Territory. They were as scarce as hen's teeth nowadays. But Funk wouldn't know that.

'How many?' he asked casually.

'Oh, maybe a dozen or less. They ain't as many these days, is there?'

O'Brien felt something release its hold slightly inside him. Some days you got bad news and good news at the same time. This didn't make up for Smitty, but it was a salve on the wound.

'Well, thanks, Funk. I'll check it out. And if you get past here again, stop in and see us.'

A moment later Funk and the aura of Fort Revenge were gone. O'Brien stood there looking after him. It was strange how things happened. If Funk hadn't run across him out here he might never have heard about the buffalo. And he realized now how lucky he had been to bring the Sharps along with him. He could take advantage of this opportunity to confront a herd for what might be the last time ever. And he wouldn't waste valuable hours returning to the cabin.

He had no hide wagon now, but the stallion could carry a couple of pelts. He walked to the horse now, slid the big gun from its scabbard, and checked its ammunition. He was ready to ride.

It took him almost two hours to find the herd. They were in a lush valley surrounded by low hills, and there was a stream a couple hundred yards away. The herd was grazing in high grass, and hadn't heard his approach. They looked peaceful and quiet. But O'Brien moistened an index finger and held it above his head, and found out that the light breeze was coming right past him to the herd. That was not good, and he figured he didn't have time to circle around and come up from the other side.

He picketed the horse with a ground stake, since there were no small trees close by. He retrieved the Sharps .500 from the horse's flank, and dropped to his knees. He would not bring the tripod, there wasn't time for that, either. Slowly he crept forward. Yard by yard. The smell of the animals coming to him lightly now. He was two hundred yards away. One-fifty.

'Careful,' he muttered to himself. 'Make this last one happen. For Shanghai.'

But in the next moment a big bull, the one closest to him and with the only robe quality pelt, got his scent.

It stopped grazing and looked right at him.

O'Brien froze in place. Seconds went past that seemed like hours. The bull couldn't see him, but still had the scent in its nostrils. It made a gutteral sound of warning, and all hell broke loose. The dozen animals started running, but had no idea which way to run. O'Brien was on one knee now, and suddenly the

Sharps boomed out and cut one of them down that hadn't decided which way to run. It dropped like a rock.

Now, though, there was lightning and thunder behind them, accompanying a dark sky, and that caused three of the herd to turn and stampede right at O'Brien.

It was obvious that two of them were going to miss him in their charge, but the third one, the big bull with the quality pelt, was going to run right over him.

O'Brien didn't flinch. Holding the big gun steady, he aimed it at the bull's muzzle as it hurtled toward him.

Thirty yards. Twenty.

The gun roared a second time and struck the buff just before it reached O'Brien. O'Brien threw the gun aside and rolled to his left just as the buffalo thundered past him, a hoof tearing at his rawhide sleeve, as it then slid to the ground on its belly, dead when it hit.

Grass was torn up all around O'Brien, and some dust filled the air. He coughed in it for a moment. His arm was bruised from the narrow escape. But he was somehow still alive.

He rose off the ground slowly, and turned to look at the big bull. It was quite a prize. The other one lay a hundred yards away in tall grass. The one that almost killed him would bring a very good price at Fort Griffin.

The bull had skidded to its death on its belly, which was just how O'Brien wanted it. Ignoring the Sharps for the moment he returned to the horse, which had miraculously not broken its picket, and brought it over to the big bull where it reared and kicked for a bit. He got some rope and a stake from his saddle roll and laid it beside the bull, where a pool of blood had gathered around the head. Taking his Bowie skinning knife from its stovepipe boot scabbard, he began cutting through skin at the neck, legs and flanks.

There was another clap of thunder nearby, but it was apparent that there would be no rain, for which he was grateful.

Now he took the stake and with a mallet, drove it through the nose of the bull and into the ground. After that he took a tuft of skin at the nape of the neck and knotted it into the end of the rope he had brought from the horse.

Now he was almost ready. He brought the stallion alongside the buffalo and secured the other end of the rope to his saddlehorn. Climbing aboard the horse then, he slowly coaxed the animal backwards and away from the head of the buffalo, and as the rope grew taut, the skin began ripping off the buff all the way to the tail.

The buffalo was skinned.

He patted the stallion's neck. It had been the horse's first time. 'There. That wasn't as hard as you thought, was it?'

Since the other buffalo was a hundred yards away, O'Brien decided to go ahead and do a scraping of the hide where it now lay. A scraper came out of a saddlebag and he worked on the hide for another hour before leaving it. There would be a second scraping at the cabin, before he laid it out in the sun for curing.

Before he left the buffalo he cut several steaks off it and wrapped them in an oil cloth for their trip back. He would share them with Ethan and Dru Purvis, and Sarah.

He removed his weathered Stetson and wiped at his brow, and was reminded how he and Smitty had done this for hours, into the night, after a big kill.

He would load the hide aboard his mount later. He went to his rife and picked it up, and stopped a moment to look up at the sky again. A flash of lightning lit up a darkened horizon, but still there was no rain, and he ignored it. The stallion had wandered a short distance away, so he decided to walk on over to the second kill to take a look at the hide.

When he got there, another lightning bolt struck in a distant stand of trees. 'I better try to get this finished up,' he mumbled to himself.

He was bending over the buff, rifle still in hand and vertical, when there was a deafening clap of thunder right overhead, with a bolt of lightning that struck the muzzle of the Sharps and traveled through it, O'Brien and the dead buffalo in a spit-instant.

O'Brien was blasted off his feet and hit the ground ten feet away, his hat and one boot gone and his rawhides smoldering.

He lay unconscious for almost a full minute, and then came round, trying to remember what happened. He coughed once, and then sat up.

'I'll be damned,' he managed. In two decades of hunting shaggies, this had never happened to him.

It took him a minute to get up. He looked at his left hand, the one that had been loosely holding the rifle. It was red and blistered. There were places on the rawhides that were scorched, and his chest underneath felt like he had gotten a sunburn.

But for the second time that day, he was still alive.

He walked over to the dead buffalo. Its hide had been burned enough to ruin it. The barrel of the Sharps had been split right down the middle, where it lay smoking on the ground.

'Well,' he said out loud, standing there. 'Maybe my last day on a shaggy hunt, and look at this.' He didn't even pick up the rifle. As he turned to find his boot and hat, a grin edged its way on to his face.

'There ain't nothing quite like it.'

FIVE

The evening before O'Brien's hazardous hunt, Wade Guthrie had taken his men to Scottville to locate and recruit Brett St Clair for his decimated gang, but had been unsuccessful. A bartender at the saloon there had repeated Guthrie's inquiry to a drifter, the drifter on his way south had told the story to R.C. Funk, and Funk mentioned it to O'Brien. So O'Brien already knew that Guthrie was trying to replenish the loss he had suffered at O'Brien's hands.

Now, at midday, while O'Brien was getting the big pelt and his equipment ready to go, the diminished gang had ridden into a small village that was south of Scottville a short distance called French Lick, where someone had seen St Clair a few days previously.

The threesome rode into town sober-faced, looking it over with obvious disdain. There was just the one street cut out of a trail west, with a couple dozen houses, a blacksmith shop, and a saloon called the Mountain View. St Clair was supposed to have an old girlfriend there.

Simon Tate squinted down the street as they surveyed the place. 'They call this a town?'

'I've been in Lakota settlements smaller than this,' Skin Walker offered, leaning on his saddlehorn.

'I ain't talking about Indians,' Tate replied caustically, spitting on the ground. 'You sure this is the place, Wade?' Low and squat, he didn't tire in the saddle like most men.

'This is the place,' Guthrie answered in his flat voice. 'Let's go in and ask about him.' He was still seething inside him about the killing of Morgan and Garrett by the hunter, and still finding it a little incredible.

They all dismounted then, and shortly found themselves inside a small, smelly saloon where a number of patrons had already gathered – a few townsfolk, and a small gathering of ranch hands from the area.

When the three entered everybody stopped talking for a moment to assess their looks, but then the small buzz of conversation continued. There was a greasy-looking bartender behind a short mahogany bar, and sawdust on the floor. He was swatting a fly on the bar surface, and there was a hanging roll of fly paper above his head, dotted with black corpses.

'What a dump!' Tate grumbled.

Guthrie led them to an unoccupied table near a wall, and after a long moment the obese bartender came over to their table with a soiled bar cloth in one hand.

'Nice to see you, strangers. Just passing through?' Guthrie gave him a look that made his mouth go slightly dry. 'Just making palaver,' he grinned uncertainly.

'Bring us a bottle of Planters Rye,' Guthrie told him. 'Unopened.'

'I can do that. Will that be all? We got boiled eggs just brought in this morning. I can even make you a ham sandwich.'

'I'm looking for a man,' Guthrie said, ignoring the questions. 'Somebody that lives hereabouts? His name is St Clair. Brett St Clair.'

The bartender screwed up his face. 'St Clair. That name sounds familiar somehow.'

At a nearby table sat three cowhands, all carrying iron, and looking tough and hard-bitten. One of them looked over at Guthrie. 'He was in here last night.' Caustically. 'What's it to you?'

Guthrie ignored the hostility. 'He's an old friend. Are you sure it was last night?'

'I said it, didn't I?' Some low laughter from his companions. 'What the hell!' Tate frowned.

'Let it go,' Guthrie said casually. 'We don't have the time.' He turned to the barkeep. 'Bring the eggs. A half-dozen.'

The other man nodded. 'I'll have it all here in the jerk of a heifer's tail.' He grinned, but got no response.

'That rye better not be watered,' Tate called after him as he left.

After the bartender was gone, the same ranch hand that had spoken to Guthrie now turned to Tate. 'You got a pretty big mouth for a little man. You better get that rye in you to quiet you down.'

70

Again, there was quiet laughter from the other table. Tate turned to them, frowning heavily. 'Little man?'

The cowboy shrugged. He was slim and well muscled, and wore a Colt Army revolver at his hip. 'Well, yeah. What are you, three or four feet? I never seen the like. Maybe your mother laid with one of them circus chimps, that could explain your shortcomings.' With emphasis on the last word.

That brought out an uproar of laughter from their table, and from some of the other nearby drinkers.

But Tate's face was suddenly red: he rose from his chair, and as he did so Walker reached and slid his Starr .44 from its holster before Tate could reach for it. That caused some more laughter.

Tate whirled on Walker. 'What the hell are you doing?' 'Keeping you out of trouble,' Guthrie answered for him. 'We've got business here. Remember?'

'You don't need the gun,' the cowpoke persisted. 'Here.' He took the Colt at his side and laid it on the table. Then he stood up and moved between the tables. 'I'm disarmed.'

Tate silently closed the distance between them. Guthrie knew that he was deceptively strong for his size, but he didn't want this. 'Tate.'

Tate wasn't listening. He was face to face with the much taller man now. 'Go ahead,' the cowpoke grinned. 'Take your best shot. If your arms can reach me.'

71

But Tate had no interest in a fair fight. Suddenly he kicked out savagely at the other man's left knee-cap, fracturing it loudly. The surprised cowboy bent double in raw pain, as Tate grabbed him by the head and neck and ran him against the bar head-first. His head smacked the hard wood loudly, and he slid to the floor, unconscious.

The entire room had fallen silent.

'Holy Mother!' the bartender muttered.

'Get him out of here,' Guthrie called to the bar-keep. 'And Tate. Get to hell back over here and try to keep out of trouble.'

Tate was still flushed. 'You heard him. He'd been dead now if you hadn't butted in. It was my business.'

'Not while you're working for me,' Guthrie retorted as squat, bow-legged Tate returned to their table.

'Save some of it for the hunter,' Walker suggested. 'It might save your life.'

'Hell. If you want me to, Wade, I'll ride out there by myself and do it for you. There ain't a buffalo man I can't take down with one shot.'

'That's what Morgan and Garrett thought,' Walker suggested.

That irritated Guthrie. 'Walker, I'm getting a little tired of hearing what a tough guy this O'Brien is. And the goddam Lakota nonsense about him. Drop it.'

Walker shrugged. 'It's only what I heard, Wade. Anyway, the badger will get us through this.'

That was even more irritating to Guthrie. 'You mention that badger just one more time, Walker, and...'

He was facing the door, and paused as he saw a tall man walk in. 'Well, I'll be damned. It's St Clair.'

The tall man saw Guthrie's table immediately, and a smile broke on to his lean face. He wore only a dark vest over a work shirt, and a dark hat, and there was a Colt Army .45 slung prominently across his belly, so it was the first thing you saw as he approached. There was a slight scar above his mouth where a cleft lip had been repaired. He came over to Guthrie's table as the bartender hauled the unconscious cowpoke to a back room. His companions rose and left, casting dark glances at Guthrie's table.

'Wade,' St Clair greeted him. 'What's that all about?'

Guthrie rose and shook his hand. 'Oh, one of the locals just gave us some trouble. It's nothing. Sit down and have a drink with us.'

St Clair took a fourth chair, and looked Tate and Walker over. His appearance was a cut above theirs, and the glance tended toward disdain.

'These are my riding partners, Brett. Tate over here, and Walker. We just did a nice little job together.'

'Wells Fargo?'

Guthrie smiled a hard smile.

'I heard you were in town and looking for me.' He gave off an aura of supreme confidence. Like Guthrie, he had never been beaten in a gunfight.

Guthrie nodded. 'I just lost some people, and I'm putting a gang back together. You and I had some times back then, and I thought you might like to join up with us.'

'For what?' St Clair wondered.

'I have some ideas. I'd like to hit one of the stage-coaches on the trail. One that carries gold. I have information on one already. After that, just about anything. I know of two small banks in the county that have no security at all. They might be easier than the coach.' 'What's the split?'

'I'm doing all the brain work. 'I'll take forty and the three of you can split the rest.'

St Clair thought about that for a minute. He had had a small gang of his own for a while, and he was accustomed to running things. But that was then, and this was now. 'I can do that,' he said.

'You won't regret it,' Walker spoke up then. 'Wade is the smartest man I've ever rode with.'

St Clair studied his face and then looked over at Tate. 'How do you get onboard a horse?'

Tate's face colored again. 'The same way you do, I'd guess.'

But Guthrie intervened. 'Tate is a good boy, Brett. You'll see, on our next job. But before that, we have a little payback to perform.'

St Clair frowned. 'Oh?'

'There's this buffalo hunter. In tight with the Birney Pass sheriff. I sent two men over there to cut him out of the equation and he killed them.'

St Clair arched his light brow. 'Both of them?'

'Both of them,' Guthrie said soberly. 'We're going back out there and do it right this time.'

'What's his name?'

'O'Brien,' Walker supplied.

'Hmm. That sounds familiar. Is he the one that lived with the Lakota for a while?'

Skin Walker grinned. 'The same.'

'I heard something about him. I can't remember what it was.'

'It wouldn't of been good,' Walker offered.

Guthrie gave him a scouring look.

'When do you want to do this?' St Clair asked.

Guthrie had already made up his mind. 'Today,' he responded bitterly. 'This afternoon.' He took a last swig of his drink. 'Right now.'

It wasn't much more than an hour later when the new gang of Guthrie arrived at O'Brien's cabin, while O'Brien was still out on the trail, resetting a couple of traps before he headed back with his prize robe-quality buffalo pelt. Unlike Morgan and Garrett, the foursome rode right up to the cabin, peering into the stable as they passed it.

'I don't see his mount anywhere,' Guthrie said darkly. 'Unless he hid it in the trees over there.'

'Well, let's go find out,' St Clair said. He had no more fear of the hunter than Guthrie. Walker, however, was sweating on his face and under his arms, and Tate was breathing shallowly.

They dismounted at a rail before the cabin, and all four approached it, Guthrie and St Clair looking all around them.

Walker drew the Joslyn .44 at his side, even though nobody else had. 'He could be waiting in there,' he said quietly to Guthrie.

Guthrie didn't understand Walker. In other situations he was aggressive and bold. But the Lakota legends had frayed his nerves. 'Get hold of yourself, Walker. If he is in there, I want you to be of some use to me.'

'I'm fine,' Walker lied.

They were at the cabin door. Guthrie nodded to the others and they drew their weapons. He unlatched the big door and shoved it open.

They were met with silence. Guthrie motioned them in, one by one, Tate going first. The big room was empty 'Goddam it,' Guthrie swore.

Walker and Tate opened two doors, to the bedroom and a utility room, looked around, and came back out.

'He ain't here,' Walker said with ill-hidden relief.

'He knew you were coming,' St Clair said. 'He's probably in town with that sheriff till this blows over.'

'He's scared of us,' Tate grinned.

When they all looked over at him soberly, the grin slid off his flat face. 'I'm so juiced I could chew nails,' Guthrie announced, his face clouded with hot anger. 'But I have no idea where to find him. We can't go confront Purvis. He might have a posse there by now.' He looked around the room. 'Burn it down. Burn it to the ground.'

St Clair looked over at him. 'What?' Walker said with a frown.

'You heard me. There's kerosene lamps here. Use them.' 'What the hell for?' Walker objected. 'All you'll do is make him very angry. How does that help us?'

'It helps me,' Guthrie growled. 'It helps make up for what he did to me.'

'It will throw him right into the sheriff's lap,' Tate suggested. 'Good!' Guthrie fairly shouted. 'Then we'll get a chance at him!'

St Clair decided to side with Guthrie. 'Wade's right, boys. If this shoves him into our path, that's right where we want him. Anyway, what can he do against us that Purvis can't?'

Guthrie's voice was cold now when he spoke. 'Incinerate it.'

Tate and Walker reluctantly nodded, remembering tales told about the hunter.

'You, Walker. Grab the lamps in here. Tate, take a look in the bedroom. And then start spreading it around.'

Guthrie and St Clair looked around the room while the other two gathered kerosene, Guthrie hoping for money or something else of value. They found nothing but O'Brien's and Sarah's personal belongings, and household goods.

In a few minutes the twosome was back with the bases of oil lamps, which contained the fuel Guthrie wanted.

'Now. Spread it liberally over everything,' Guthrie ordered them. 'And save a little for outside.'

They set to work with Guthrie watching them. The smelly liquid was emptied on to O'Brien's buffalo skin rug, and an old skinning knife on a shelf that Shanghai Smith had given him when he and Sarah left Fort Revenge. It was dumped on to a cupboard that contained all of Sarah's special dinnerware and cutlery. On a different shelf, they threw some on to the row of books that Sarah had brought all the way from Boston.

Guthrie looked around and was pleased. 'All right, let's get outside. I want to put some on the base of the walls out there.'

He hadn't thought of the utility room because it seemed unimportant to him. But outside the two underlings dumped the rest of the kerosene on the base of the cabin until it was gone.

'Walker, you stay here till we get the horses down the slope. Then light a match to it.'

'Why me?' Walker complained.

'Because you seem to need it,' Guthrie answered without explanation.

Walker gave him a dark look. Some day after Guthrie had made him rich, he would find him asleep some night and slide a Lakota knife through his eye.

The other three unhitched the horses and led them well away from the cabin. When Walker saw they were safe, he took a match from his pocket and threw it at the base of the cabin. Nothing happened. He swore and took out a second one. This time a flame erupted down by the ground and quickly traveled up the side of the cabin.

Walker joined his comrades to watch at a distance, a glum look on his narrow, Indian-looking face. As they all stood watching, the cabin was slowly engulfed in flame, with a crackling and roaring. In just moments the blaze was reaching for the sky, thirty feet above the cabin, with black smoke occluding the view of the snow peaks behind it.

They had all remounted their horses now, and Guthrie sat his with a grim smile on his square face.

'Jesus,' Tate murmured.

'Take that, you sonofabitch,' Guthrie hissed out with extreme satisfaction. He let out a long breath. 'All right, boys. Let's ride.'

***

O'Brien had been riding home all through the occurrence at his cabin, without any thought of Guthrie. He had decided that, because of the buffalo steaks in his saddlebags, he would make a special trip in to Birney Pass the next day to share them with Sarah and the Purvises. In the meantime, he would give the buffalo robe its second and final scraping, and hang it out in the sun to cure. It would bring a handsome price at market, and allow Sarah to visit the general store in town for some personal luxury items. That pleased him.

He was beginning to think of Sarah's pregnancy more and more as it came closer to 'her time'. His main hope, after Sarah's getting through it all right, was that it would be a boy. Feelings of parenthood, which would have been entirely foreign to him as little as a year ago, were gradually creeping into his subconscious, giving him an unexpected, pleasant anticipation about what was soon going to happen.

He could see himself teaching a son how to shoot, and hunt and trap. Show him how to track like an Apache, and stalk like a cougar. Things his own father had taught him, back in the Shenandoah Valley in Virginia.

His father had been a big man, like O'Brien, and was an immigrant Highlander Scot who was apparently running from something back home, since the name O'Brien was an alias for him. O'Brien's Welsh mother was a stout but good-looking woman who gave him the Welsh Christian name of Badrig, which he hated and never used. Sarah knew it, but never reminded him of it.

It was still a beautiful day in late afternoon as O'Brien neared home. There was scattered snow on the distant peaks, and in these foothills there was grass that the breeze moved in waves, like the ocean, and there were wildflowers whose redolence sweetened the air.

His first indication that all might not be well on this pleasant day was when he crested a small rise of ground and saw the distant sky darkened by black smoke. He reined in abruptly, realizing that it was coming from the direction of his cabin. He frowned. 'What the hell?'

The stallion snorted softly, catching his new mood. He patted its neck, staring. It didn't look like a wildfire. It was too concentrated.

He spurred the horse on, and kept his eyes on the horizon. After another half-hour, he crested another small swell of ground, and saw the cabin.

He reined the horse in sharply, and just stared soberly at the ugly sight.

There were no flames now. There were just embers beneath the thinning smoke, and the ruins of his cabin in the midst of that.

He slumped in his saddle, staring unbelieving at what had been their home. The pleasure of his hunt evaporated in a moment.

'You bastard,' he said from his throat. 'You demon from hell.'

His reaction had been outwardly subdued, almost quiet. But a new and deep hatred for Wade Guthrie was growing inside him as he sat there. The hunter was not an emotional man. But he was feeling a boiling inside him that he had never felt before. It had taken him months to rebuild that trapper's cabin and make it a real home for his new wife. And in one moment a vile thing like Guthrie had taken it away from him. And from Sarah.

My God, Sarah. How could he break this to her, in her condition? He dismounted and hitched the stallion to a scorched hitching rail.

Then he scanned the horizon to make sure he was alone. The horse made a sound in its throat.

'It's all right,' he said heavily. 'Everything will be all right.'

He walked up to the ruins. The big front door had collapsed, and there were no standing walls except at the extreme end of the ruins. He picked up a length of charred wood to use as a tool, battered some debris from his path, and stood in the midst of the remains.

He was in what had been their combined parlor and kitchen, and there was nothing but burnt trash and ashes. He saw a thick pile of stuck-together ash that had been Sarah's books. Wading through hot debris, he went on into the area of their bedroom, and the big bed lay completely destroyed on the floor, a smoldering mess.

Nothing of value remained.

O'Brien stood there and let a deep sigh issue from the depths of him. He remembered that, even before he had traveled south to the Indian Territory, he had used the trapper's cabin for a whole winter and spring, until the beaver ran out.

He had caught a crooked town marshal from Birney Pass trying to steal his pelts one day in this cabin, and there had been a gunfight that had ended in the marshal's death. That confrontation was one of the reasons he had decided he had better leave the area for a while.

He had thought that kind of thing was an anomaly in these foothills, and that it was a relatively safe place to bring a young woman to live with him.

He had been wrong.

The memory of those early days here reminded O'Brien of the utility room at the far end of the cabin. That part had seemed relatively undamaged from outside. He waded through heavy debris across the wide area that had been the main living quarters and to a partially destroyed doorway to the small, farthest room. When he got there he pushed some charred wood aside with his burnt stick, and saw that most of the things in there were intact. Traps, boxes of ammunition that hadn't exploded, ground sheets, saddlery, and miscellaneous items. There was also a stack of hides. Some of it smelled of fire, but that was temporary.

O'Brien had a job ahead of him. For the next two hours he hauled everything usable outside and stacked it into a pile, then found two unburnt logs from the utility room section and made himself a travois to haul the things behind the stallion for the ride into town. Some of the pelts he fastened aboard the horse, to balance the weight of the big buffalo hide on the other side.

When he attached the travois to the horse's saddlery it balked and protested for a moment or two. But with his reassurance it quietened down and accepted its new responsibility.

A short time later O'Brien was on his way to town. He never looked back at the cabin.

SIX

When Wade Guthrie's gang returned from destroying O'Brien's cabin, he surprised them with another announcement. The stagecoach he intended to rob was coming through that very afternoon. He had decided not to break the news until they had finished the mission to the cabin, so nobody would be objecting to doing that first.

While O'Brien was starting out slowly toward Birney Pass, therefore, the gang was arriving at a pre-selected site on the stage trail west of their hideout, and of Scottville. Guthrie took them up on to a rocky slope above the trail, where they could hide behind large boulders and see the coach coming from a distance.

They had dismounted and picketed the horses near them, and were now sitting on the ground in a loose circle, with Walker standing near them where he could keep a lookout on the trail. They were a half-hour early, and relaxed. Guthrie was still self-satisfied about what they had done at the cabin. Walker, however, felt just the opposite, but hid that from Guthrie.

'I hit a stage down in Kansas once,' St Clair said, sitting there looking out over the slope. 'We thought there was gold aboard there, too. But when we opened the bank box, there was just municipal bonds and legal papers. We were so damned mad we shot the driver, the shotgun man, and the lone passenger.'

Walker glanced over at him from his lookout position.

'I shot a man in a saloon once because he gave me a wrong look,' Guthrie reminisced, taking the Schofield .45 from its holster and turning it over in his hand. He treated it as if it were a part of himself, like an arm or leg. He had not kept count of the deaths that sidearm had caused, but it was many. It had been in double figures even before he was fired from the Texas Rangers.

'I went to one of them medicine shows once, over in Arizona,' Tate put in, leaning against a boulder near St Clair. 'They had the head of Geronimo pickled in a jar. You had to pay fifty cents to see it. I spent my money and took a look.'

'How was it?' St Clair grinned.

'Ugly,' Tate said, making a face. 'It was all bloated up so you didn't know what you was looking at.'

Walker frowned, from a short distance. 'What the hell did you expect, for God's sake. Pickled in a goddam jar.'

They all just looked toward him for a moment, and said nothing. 'Why the hell would you want to see that?' Walker finally added, shaking his head.

Tate grunted out a laugh. 'Oh, yeah. The champion of the red man. I forgot.'

'Tate,' Guthrie said.

'Yeah?'

'Drop it.'

Tate looked away, dour-faced.

'Hold it, everybody,' Walker said quickly. 'I see dust out there. I think we're about to have company.'

They were on their feet in a moment. Guthrie joined Walker and peered into the distance. 'Yes. That's it. Everybody mount up.'

In the next few minutes the four riders came out on to the trail to watch the stagecoach approach, then there was some excitement as the driver saw them and tried to stop his team. The coach slid to a halt twenty yards away, kicking up a cloud of dust that almost blocked their view of it briefly.

There were two men on the box, and one carried a shotgun. The shotgun was aimed at the gang.

'Do you want to live?' Guthrie shouted at him. No response.

'If you do, throw down. Otherwise, not one of you will leave here alive.'

'Play it smart, boys!' St Clair followed up. 'You don't owe that bank nothing! Save yourselves!'

The shotgun man fired the big gun with an explosion that made the ears ring, and struck Simon Tate in the face and almost tore his head off. He was thrown off his mount as the driver raised his whip to the team. But in mid-action Walker fired his Joslyn .44 and hot lead hit the driver hard in center chest.

86

He was punched back against the coach, and then slumped on his seat, dead. The shotgun rider now tried to draw a Colt sidearm, but both Guthrie and St Clair now fired at once, and he was hit in the belly and the face, Guthrie's shot shattering his nose and sending shards of it into his skull. He was knocked off the coach and was dead before he hit the ground.

The team of horses reared and plunged, but did not run. Guthrie was swearing under his breath as he glanced at Tate on the ground. There was nothing about his face that was recognizable.

The three of them walked their mounts up to the stage, and Walker took control of the team. A moment later three passengers emerged from inside, their hands up.

'Don't shoot us!' an older-looking fellow called out. 'You can have everything we've got!'

There was another, younger man and a boy of about twelve. Guthrie just stared at them without speaking. But he was boiling inside. 'Is there gold in that box up there?' he finally addressed the man who had spoken.

'We don't know! They don't tell us nothing!'

Guthrie motioned to St Clair. He dismounted, went over to the coach, and climbed up on to the buckboard. He grabbed the dead driver and threw him off to the ground. Then he was opening a lid on the buckboard and looking inside. He pulled out a small box and climbed down with it.

Now Guthrie and Walker were on the ground, too. Guthrie shot a small lock off it, and looked inside. He opened two cloth bags, and there were gold coins in one and silver in the other.

He looked up with a small grin. 'Jackpot!' St Clair returned the grin.

'Put it aboard your mount,' Guthrie told Walker. They had brought a special carrier for it.

Walker and St Clair carried the box to Walker's horse while Guthrie walked over to the passengers, who were pale and frightened. The boy was trembling inside.

'Who are you people?' Guthrie asked genially.

'Why, I'm Jethro Cates,' the older man said, swallowing hard. 'I own a little ranch down the trail here. And this is my nephew and his boy.'

Guthrie nodded. 'How was the ride today? Rough trail?'

'It was an easy trip,' the younger man spoke up. Guthrie leveled a look on him. 'Did I ask you?' The fellow hesitated. 'No.'

'My dad can talk when he wants to,' the boy broke in. He licked dry lips.

Guthrie settled his gaze on the youngster for a moment. Then he aimed the Schofield at his father and casually shot him in the chest. The fellow flew backwards as if jerked on a lariat, and hit the ground ten feet away.

A loud scream came from the boy.

St Clair and Walker looked over at Guthrie in surprise. Guthrie aimed his gun at the boy, who was crying now.

'Hey!' Walker objected.

Guthrie lowered the sidearm. 'Yes?'

'Well, what the hell, Wade?'

Guthrie just stared at him coldly for a moment. Then he turned to St Clair, who had observed the exchange with interest. 'Put both of them back aboard.'

The older man had an arm over the boy's shoulder, trying to comfort him. But he felt relief when he heard that order by Guthrie. He helped the boy aboard and got in himself.

'You're going to take a little ride,' Guthrie was saying pleasantly. When they were seated inside, he turned to Walker. 'Do it,' he growled.

Both Walker and St Clair regarded him curiously. Then Walker's face went grim. 'Hell, no. I already shot a woman for you at the depot. The spirit told me that was wrong. I will not kill a kid.'

Tension crackled in the air around them.

'Do you understand, in that tiny brain of yours,' Guthrie finally said quietly, 'that the boy can identify all of us?'

'I'll talk to him. Get a promise.'

St Clair sighed heavily. 'Never mind, Wade,' he said. He walked over to the coach, aimed one of his Colts inside, and fired twice.

Walker let out a long sigh. 'Sonofabitch.'

Guthrie nodded his assent to St Clair, and turned to Walker. 'Have your Lakota spirits given you a conscience, Walker? Remember, "Man hath no pre-eminence over the beasts, for all is vanity".'

Walker looked sullen.

'You go against me again, Indian man, and you'll pay the price. And it's too late in the game to just fire you. Understand?'

Walker understood the threat well. He got himself under control. 'I'll carry my load, Wade.'

'Good. You and Brett get those other bodies aboard. But not Tate. Haul him over behind that big boulder over there.'

They finished all of that in just a few minutes. Guthrie then went to a horse at the lead of the team, and slapped it on the rump, and the stagecoach jolted ahead and was roaring on down the trail in a heavy cloud of dust.

'That will give them a little surprise at the next stop,' Guthrie grinned to himself. He had no feelings at all about what he had done. He just did not have it in him. 'Let's mount up and get to hell out of here. We got Christmas back at the cabin.'

***

It was almost dark when O'Brien reined up in front of the sheriff's office in Birney Pass.

It had been a hard ride, lugging that saved material behind him on the makeshift carrier. His chest and face burned from the lightning strike, and his left hand had blistered up. He sat wearily in his saddle for several moments before he dismounted, and then suddenly Ethan Purvis was emerging from the front door, a look of curiosity on his lean face.

'O'Brien! What the hell is going on, boy?'

'Ethan. This is stuff from our cabin. I was hoping you could find a place to keep it for us for a while.'

Purvis was looking him over. 'Sure, I can do that. I got an equipment shed out back that will hold that. But why are you bringing it here, amigo? And why is the left side of your face all red?' He saw that O'Brien had been careful of his left hand, and glanced at it. 'And blisters on your palm there?'

O'Brien sighed. 'It ain't nothing, Ethan. I got in the way of a lightning hit. It will all heal quick. That ain't the bad news.'

Purvis regarded him soberly. 'Maybe we better step inside.'

When they got in there, they sat at Purvis' old desk. On an opposite wall was a poster board with wanted dodgers on it, and one of them was for the Guthrie gang. There was already a reward for each member, with a very big one on Guthrie himself. O'Brien had been in dozens of such rooms.

'You got some scorching on your rawhides, too,' Purvis remarked.

'I'm going to walk you down to the doc, the one that's seeing Sarah.'

'I don't want no doctor,' O'Brien told him. 'I been stung by wasps worse than this.'

Purvis suppressed a smile. But then his face went sober again. 'Now. Give me the bad news, partner.'

O'Brien met his eyes. 'Our cabin is gone.'

Purvis was stunned. 'What the hell do you mean?'

O'Brien studied the wall behind Purvis for a moment. 'It was burned. Burned to the ground.

91

I think you can guess who did it. I saw the prints of their horses on the slope.'

Purvis slammed his hand on to the desk, angrily. 'That sub-human animal Guthrie!'

'He must of come back to kill me. When he saw I wasn't there, he thought it would be a good idea to take my home·. The only real one I've had since leaving Virginia. That cabin had been there for a decade, in one form or another. And Sarah had made it look so homey.'

O'Brien shook his head slowly. 'Sarah. How do I tell Sarah? And in her condition.'

Purvis blew his cheeks out. 'I see what you mean. But there's no way to avoid it, is there?'

'No. She'll have to know. It's going to hurt her bad, Ethan.'

'We'll all be there with her,' Purvis said somberly.

After that sit-down Purvis helped O'Brien move the things from the cabin into the shed out in back of the office. Then, with O'Brien fighting him every moment, Purvis got him to the doctor, who put salve on O'Brien's face, chest and hand, and placed a bandage across the hand.

'That can come off in a few days,' the doctor told him as Purvis watched.

'We'll be lucky if it's on there tomorrow,' Purvis grinned.

'How's Sarah doing, Doc?' O'Brien asked him.

'Oh, she's coming along just like we expected,' he responded. Sarah had asked him not to mention the difficulty to anybody. Especially not O'Brien. 'Say, incidentally, that's one good-looking woman you got yourself there, mister.'

O'Brien didn't respond.

'We're all very taken with her,' Purvis answered for him.

When they got outside O'Brien flexed the left hand with the bandage. 'Is that boy really any good? I mean, with woman stuff.'

'Oh, yes,' Purvis assured him. 'He's the best doctor in five counties. And there's Olivia too. She's already seen Sarah once.'

'I never worried over nothing before,' O'Brien muttered. 'But this is different.'

'Of course,' Purvis said.

'I never had to think on anything that didn't affect me,' O'Brien went on. 'For my whole life. Now – now I'd lay down in the path of a stampeding herd for that girl.'

Purvis smiled. 'I think she probably knows that.'

'We don't even have a place to lay our heads down,' O'Brien said. 'And there'll be three of us pretty soon.'

'Well, at least that's easy to solve,' Purvis told him. 'You'll just move in with Sarah and stay right with us till this is all over. You'll make Dru very happy.'

'I hate to trouble you.'

'Trouble, hell. You'll be good to have around.' He wanted to recruit him for action against Guthrie. He knew of the atrocities at the depot and on the stage trail, and realized the county was being terrorized by very bad men. O'Brien had already rejected his offer, but he wondered if it would be different now.

They arrived at Purvis's house at just after dark. Sarah and Dru were in the kitchen trying to make a supper prepared earlier survive Purvis' late arrival. When they heard the front door open and close they came into the big parlor together. Dru reacted first.

'Ethan! Where did you find this fellow?'

But then Sarah was focusing on O'Brien. She went over to him. 'My God. What happened to you? Your face. And your hand.'

O'Brien was already tired of explaining it. 'A lightning bolt found me, Sarah. Out hunting. It ain't nothing. I run on to a herd, and got us a nice buffalo pelt.'

'Buffalo pelt?' she said irritably. 'Look at you!' She fell against him and laid her head on his chest, her eyes moist.

O'Brien hugged her belly to him, enjoying it. 'Hey. I'm fit as a newborn colt. Really.'

'I took him to your doc,' Purvis said. 'He said he'll be just fine in a couple of days. He's going to stay with us tonight.'

Sarah took his bandaged hand in hers, and then looked up at him. 'Some days I wish you would take up a less interesting life,' she said softly.

'I don't think he's the type to live a normal, civilized life,' Dru offered bluntly. But was immediately sorry, because of Sarah.

'I offered him a regular job,' Purvis reminded them.

O'Brien gave him a sober look.

'O'Brien had a job. In Fort Revenge,' Sarah said. 'Really?' Dru said rather too incredulously.

Purvis frowned. He was unstrapping his gunbelt. 'This hombre? Actually working for somebody?'

'It was his best friend,' Sarah said. 'Shanghai Smith.'

The news from R.C. Funk crashed in on O'Brien again. He hoped Sarah didn't see his reaction.

'And he didn't work for him,' Sarah continued. 'They were partners in a stage line. But Smitty also went out trapping with him regularly. If he hadn't had that, I doubt he would have attempted it. Anyway, after a short time he couldn't do it any more. He called it the call of the coyote moon.' She smiled at O'Brien.

Purvis laughed. 'That figures. I never met a buffalo man that could handle town life. And this one is the worst of them.' He excused himself then to go wash up.

'Smitty is one of the best friends I ever made,' Sarah reminisced, standing there with an arm still around her husband.

O'Brien sighed slightly. 'He was the best man on a herd I ever seen,' he said quietly. He hadn't mentioned Smitty or the cabin yet.

Sarah glanced up at him again because of the way he had said it. 'Well,' Dru intervened, 'if you found a herd in these parts, you ought to take up professional gambling, O'Brien.' A small laugh.

'O'Brien was the best at what he did,' Sarah said, looking at his hand again. 'Does that hurt?'

O'Brien frowned lightly, as if not understanding the question. 'Oh. Why, I don't even remember why the damn bandage is on there.' Sarah smiled at Dru. 'He doesn't feel pain like the rest of us.'

Dru laughed in her throat. 'Why doesn't that surprise me?' she said drily. 'Well, Mr Hunter, we can fix you right up in Sarah's room tonight. But now we got to go in and eat while it's still eatable.'

A few minutes later they were all seated at the big kitchen table as they had been when O'Brien brought Sarah to them. It was pot roast now, and O'Brien ate ravenously, making Dru stop and watch him for a moment, with a satisfied smile.

When they were all just about finished, Ethan Purvis looked across the table to O'Brien. 'Guthrie has been busy again.'

O'Brien sat back on his chair. The very mention of Guthrie now touched him darkly on a gut level. 'What now?'

'He stopped a stage out on the trail west of Scottville. They killed the driver, the shotgun man, and three passengers.' He paused, wondering whether to go on. 'One of the passengers was just a kid.'

Sarah gasped slightly without knowing it.

'Good Jesus!' Dru exclaimed, her face showing shock. Purvis hadn't given her any details until that moment.

O'Brien just sat there absorbing that silently.

'Sheriffs around this area recognize that as his method of operation,' Purvis went on. 'When he does a job, he gets rid of everybody that could identify them later.' He looked around the table. 'He's very efficient.'

'He's a man without a conscience,' O'Brien commented as if to himself. 'I've run into them. On the trail.'

Purvis took a breath in and studied O'Brien's face. 'So far this is all happening in my county. So it's my responsibility.'

'That's not true!' Dru objected. 'He won't just limit himself to this county. You could get help from other lawmen hereabouts.'

He smiled at her. 'That won't work, Dru. Unless he gives them trouble too. My deputy is worthless, and I tried to get up a posse to go out and look for him. One old man, Seger, volunteered. If I took him he'd shoot hisself in the foot.'

He was addressing himself to O'Brien.

'You don't need no posse,' O'Brien suddenly spoke up. All three of the others stared at him.

'Why not?' Purvis finally asked curiously.

O'Brien turned to Sarah soberly. 'Sarah. Guthrie come back for me.'

'What?' Her lovely face full of fear.

'I wasn't there. So he burned our cabin down.'

'Oh my God!' Dru muttered.

Sarah stared at O'Brien as if he had just slapped her in the face.

She swallowed hard, and touched her belly. She looked as if she might fall off her chair. 'Oh. Oh, dear.'

'You all right?' O'Brien half-whispered to her.

She hesitated, then nodded. Dru and Purvis were watching her face. 'I'll build it up again,' O'Brien was saying. 'Better than before. We'll need more room soon anyway.'

Sarah looked over at him, then leaned her head against his shoulder. 'I'm so sorry, honey,' Dru managed.

'I'm all right,' Sarah said softly. 'As long as I have him.'

Purvis pressed his lips together. 'This might be a bad time to bring this up. But I'm not responsible for the timing. I could use some help finding Guthrie and bringing him to justice. I want to see the bastard hang.' O'Brien was staring at his plate. 'That ain't going to happen.'

Once again all three regarded him curiously. 'What the hell are you saying?' Purvis wondered.

O'Brien held his gaze. 'I'm saying I'll take care of it.' Sarah turned to him quickly, without speaking.

'Well, of course,' Purvis said. "You'll ride with me. Together we'll bring him down.'

O'Brien shook his head. 'You wear a badge, Sheriff. You have to play by the rules. Guthrie doesn't, and neither do I. Anyway, I've always worked alone. I like it that way.'

Sarah grabbed his arm. 'O'Brien. Please don't. Think of me. Think of us. I can deal with the loss of the cabin. You and I are still together. I couldn't handle it if we weren't.'

'You can't go off by yourself like that!' Dru said loudly. 'You could be breaking the law! Ethan might have to arrest you!'

Nobody paid any attention. O'Brien turned to Sarah. 'It's our cabin he burned down, Sarah. And I don't want to depend on somebody else to make that right. Anyway, he has a grudge against me now. He'll find me again, Sarah. Or he might find you and the baby when I'm not there.'

Sarah's eyes were filled with tears. She knew you couldn't oppose O'Brien when he had made up his mind on something.

'At least wait till I deliver,' she tried.

O'Brien sighed. 'And how many more women and kids will that soulless thing have murdered by then?' O'Brien suggested.

Sarah had no answer. She laid her head on his shoulder again. Dru looked at her husband and saw the resignation in his eyes.

She turned to Sarah, trying to think of something positive to say.

'It will be all right, darling. I wouldn't want him coming after me.' Nobody responded to that.

They didn't think it was required.

SEVEN

No further word was spoken of the Guthrie matter at the Purvis house, either that evening or the following morning. Sarah couldn't go to sleep, and kept looking over at the figure of O'Brien beside her in bed.

Remembering.

One memory after another came sidling across her consciousness, like slides from a candle projector: the first time she had ever laid eyes on him, when she was sitting on the buckboard of a disabled cones-toga holding a Boston parasol over her head, hoping the Pawnee, who had killed her two drivers while she hid safely nearby, did not return. The sudden sound of O'Brien's appaloosa, and her frightened scream before she got a look at him. His quick reassurance, and him burying her drivers while she gratefully watched him, and then having a tin of peaches together, from the wagon's cargo.

More memories came pushing in. O'Brien saving her from a hungry grizzly, and without killing it, which surprised her. Her learning that he had recently killed two men who had murdered his hunting partner, and trying to fit that into her assessment of him.

In that dark bedroom, she moved over so her body was touching his. She gently ran a hand through his thick, slightly graying hair. He moved in his sleep, but did not wake. Before they ever got to Fort Revenge, where she was to meet a would-be groom, and O'Brien would seek out his old hunting partner Smith, more Pawnee came into their camp and wanted to take her as tribute for their passage, and O'Brien stopped that cold in a way she never quite understood. Later, in town, he had had to protect her from the would-be groom who turned out to be an outlaw.

There were many more memories like that, of experiences that had bonded them more tightly than O'Brien understood, until he came to her unexpectedly and asked her to come with him when he returned here.

Before she knew it, there was the light of dawn creeping in through a nearby window, and Sarah couldn't remember sleeping at all.

A couple of hours later, when O'Brien left with Purvis, Sarah kissed him goodbye on three separate occasions without knowing she had repeated it.

'Please take care of yourself,' she pleaded with him. 'For all we've been to each other. And for what will be.'

O'Brien hugged her to him. 'Has anybody ever taken me down yet?'

She hesitated. 'No.'

'Then concentrate on your situation – who knows, I might be back here in time to see it happen.'

'I'll be expecting you,' she said, her eyes moist.

He and Purvis then rode down to Purvis's office, where O'Brien went into his belongings and retrieved some ammo and a tarpaulin groundsheet. Before he left, O'Brien sat down at Purvis's desk with him briefly, at Purvis's request. With O'Brien impatient to be off.

'Why don't you reconsider all this?' Purvis began. 'Two of us working together can do better than one man against that nest of vipers.'

'I told you why.'

'Then maybe we could coordinate our efforts. You tell me where you'll start looking, and I'll cover some other area.'

O'Brien gave him a sober look. 'Ethan, you go where you want and do what you have to do. I don't care. I'm heading to Culver Junction, if that makes any difference to you.' He caught Purvis's eye. 'But I'd keep out of it, if I was you. Without a posse, you could end up dead with Guthrie standing over you.'

'And you won't?'

O'Brien sighed. 'How long you had this job, Ethan?'

Purvis frowned. 'Just over a year. But I been around a while, you know. I can use this Colt pretty good.'

'I doubt you ever been up against a Guthrie,' O'Brien said. 'Now, I'm sorry if we see different on this, Sheriff. But I'm riding out now. Alone. Unless you got something else.'

'You are a stubborn sonofabitch,' Purvis muttered soberly.

'I've heard that,' O'Brien responded. He started to get up.

'Wait a minute,' Purvis stopped him. 'Do you know anything about those two that are still with him, now that they lost one at the stagecoach?'

'I don't even know anything about Guthrie. All I have to know, I'll probably find out when I come face to face with them.'

'I've always thought it pays to know your enemy,' Purvis said.

O'Brien regarded him impatiently. 'Go ahead. I'll give you five minutes.'

Purvis studied the wall behind O'Brien. 'You already know their names. The one called Skin Walker is part Sioux. The word is he thinks he has supernatural powers. Hell, maybe he does. But he's lightning fast with that Josyn .44 he carries. If you confront more than one of them, I'd take him out first.'

O'Brien sighed. 'Go on.'

'His other man now is a new recruit.' O'Brien recalled Funk telling him about that. 'That's St Clair. I think his first name might be Brett. He wears two Colt Army .45s, and when he was younger, he won a couple awards for shooting.' He stopped, and watched O'Brien's face.

'Is that it?'

'No, there's Guthrie.' He paused, and sighed. 'This character isn't in charge by accident. He's smart as hell. The Texas Rangers have a whole file on him.

They slowly found out what he was, and fired him when he went into an outlaw's cabin one fine day and found his quarry there. He didn't arrest the man. He shot him up real good. Then he shot his wife and a grown son, who had never crossed the law in their lives.'

O'Brien shook his head. 'Just like he's doing here.'

'The thing is, he's ruthless, O'Brien. And he already hates your guts. He's good with his gun. But he'll kill you any way he can.'

O'Brien nodded. 'That figures. Now, is the lecture about over, Sheriff?'

Purvis smiled. He hadn't known the hunter very long, but he liked him very much. And he and Dru both loved Sarah. He rose, and so did O'Brien. Purvis assessed him, standing there in his rawhides and looking very wild and primitive.

'Are you as good with that Winchester as everybody says you are?'

'Oh, most of that is bull-pucky,' O'Brien frowned.

'I'll bet.' With a wry smile. 'You sure I can't talk you into a sidearm? You never know when it might help.'

'No, nursie, you can't,' O'Brien said acidly. 'Now, I'll see you when it's over. I hope it's not sooner.'

'We'll see,' Purvis told him. 'In the meantime, vaya con Dios.' Five minutes later, O'Brien was gone.

***

The next day at Guthrie's hideout cabin, the three outlaws were gathered around the crude table in the center of the room. They had just eaten a light lunch, and their plates were still there. Walker was picking a tooth with the usual paring knife.

Guthrie watched him with disgust. But he was very content inside. They had counted and divided the loot from the stagecoach, and it was considerable. Guthrie's share would support him comfortably for years to come. He expected to deposit it in a Denver bank at the earliest opportunity.

St Clair and Walker were also pleased with their new riches. St Clair had not told Guthrie, but after another successful job he intended to leave Guthrie and enjoy the fruits of his recent enterprises in a pretty little village in central Mexico, where the tequila was unwatered and the girls were willing, dark-eyed sweethearts.

Skin Walker also had post-Guthrie ideas. He was acquainted with a Lakota chief called Two Bears, who had no idea how Walker had spent the last couple of years. Walker intended to go to him and ask to be invited into the tribe, as a kind of medicine man. He could end up with more power there than the chief, if he played his cards just right. He could be a big man. He could be important.

'I'm going to let things cool off a bit now,' Guthrie was telling them. 'That Birney Pass sheriff probably has a posse put together by now. He'll come looking for us. I think if we just hunker down here for a while, he could look for a year and not find us.'

'It is not him you have to worry about,' Walker said in his slight Lakota accent.

Guthrie frowned at him. He was becoming dissatisfied with the half-breed. 'Who? That illiterate buffalo man?'

Walker grunted. 'He wouldn't be coming here to read one of your books, Wade,' he said sourly. 'He will be very single-minded, in my opinion. You burnt his cabin down. And Morgan and Garrett might have mistreated that wife of his. I hear she's pretty good to look at.' He caught Guthrie's gaze. 'I'd be pretty upset by all that. I can't even imagine how steamed up he might be in that cave-man head.'

'Cave man?' Guthrie said acidly.

Walker smiled. He liked it that he knew more about something than arrogant Guthrie. 'That's right. You're not dealing with no civilized man here, boys. This hunter has spent his whole life on the trail. He's seldom been in a town. This wife thing is new to him. He's never carried iron, but gunslingers keep out of his way. He used to wear a beard, and with that long hair, he looked more like a bear than a man. I've talked to men that have run into him. At the Fort Garland Rendezvous. He's a fair dealer, but never gets into conversation with anybody. His whole life, you understand, has been hunting and killing. And it wasn't all buffalo. Two Bears says if you go up against him, you're probably going to regret it.'

There was a long silence after that summary.

'I'm just saying what I've heard,' Walker finally added. 'I've never met him personally.'

Guthrie was irritated. 'Every time that hunter's name comes up, you make him sound like some goddam demigod. You said he doesn't even carry a sidearm. How the hell can he defend himself against a Schofield? Or that Joslyn of yours?"

Walker shrugged. 'I'm just sorry you burned that cabin. That's all I'm saying.'

St Clair hadn't spoken a word. He leaned forward on his chair. 'I've heard about this boy. They say he can hit a buffalo in the eye at five hundred yards at midnight. Most of it is probably peyote smoke. Anyway, as you say, Wade. Distance shooting expertise can't help you in a face-to-face. Any one of us here could put a couple in him before he could find the trigger on that long gun. What is it, a Henry?' 'Winchester,' Walker said. 'And he's as good with that as the Sharps he hunts with. He takes it everywhere with him.'

Guthrie glared toward a far wall. 'I hope to hell it's me gets first crack at him. He makes my gut boil, after what he did to Morgan and Garrett.'

'What he did to Morgan and Garrett is something to think on,' Walker suggested. 'I'm going to find another badger. I might need the spirits to protect me in this situation." He saw the scowl grow on Guthrie's face. 'Sorry, Wade. I forgot.'

Guthrie sat forward, too. 'You're the fastest gun I know, Indian. But you're turning into a goddam lily liver. Shape up or I'll put a bullet behind your ear while you're sleeping some night.'

Walker absorbed that somberly. He believed him.

'Now. Let's discuss something that actually has some importance to us. As I said, we'll lay off for a little while. Try to figure out what the law hereabouts is going to do about the jobs we've already done.'

107

'We could move on, Wade,' St Clair said. 'There's a big stage company out of Laramie. That would take us out of this jurisdiction, and Purvis.'

'I've thought about that,' Guthrie replied. 'But I have a couple ideas for right here in state before we spread our wings.'

'Wells Fargo again?' St Clair wondered.

'No,' Guthrie grinned. 'Banks.'

'Banks?' Walker said in surprise.

'Why not?' Guthrie said. 'I know they have new safes nowadays, with those combination locks. But Jesse James showed us how to get into them. You don't have to blow the safe. You just have to make the manager understand it's a matter of life or death. His life or his death.'

'It's more dangerous than robbing stages,' St Clair countered. 'They have alarm systems that get the law involved in just minutes.'

Guthrie nodded. 'I haven't gone into this blind, Brett. I know of two small banks within riding distance of us. They don't have alarms yet. We can be in and out before any trouble comes at us. But of course, it would be the same as usual. We couldn't leave anyone alive.'

Walker frowned. 'There could be a half-dozen bank people inside,' he said. 'And customers, even.'

St Clair looked over at Guthrie to see his reaction to that.

Guthrie was scowling. 'We'd go just when the bank is closing up for the day, and wait till all customers are gone. Anyway, what if we did have to shoot a customer? You're giving me a goddam headache, Walker.'

'We'll hope to keep the shooting to a minimum,' St Clair offered, to keep the peace. 'We could even wait till some of the employees had left.' Glancing at Guthrie for his approval.

'Hell, yes,' Guthrie grumbled. 'Anyway, we'll check both of them out in the next week or so. Familiarize ourselves. Any questions?' Giving Walker a dark look.

'None,' St Clair said quickly.

Walker sighed. 'I'm on board, Wade.'

***

O'Brien arrived in Culver Junction later that day, after several hours of riding. He hitched the stallion outside a saloon called the Culver Pass and climbed steps to a weather-beaten façade.

Inside it was quiet, because of the time of day. There were a few patrons at scattered tables, drinking quietly, and a hard-looking bartender behind a mahogany bar. A few drinkers glanced at O'Brien, and went back to talking among themselves. O'Brien walked over to the bar and ordered a Planters Rye whiskey.

The bartender didn't look up from a Billings newspaper lying in front of him. 'We don't have Planters.'

O'Brien frowned. 'Well then, what the hell do you have?'

'There's a paper on the wall back there that lists them.' Still reading.

O'Brien had brought his Winchester in with him, as usual. It was hanging under his arm. He now laid it on the bar, over the newspaper.

'Hey!' From the barkeep. Then he focused on the tall man before him. 'Oh, Christ. A mountain man. I should of known. Take that gun off my bar, mister. We got rules in here.'

'I'm asking once more. What brand of hogwash you got back there?' 'I told you. There's a list. Or can't you read?' A low chuckle.

With his free left hand O'Brien grabbed the other man by a soiled apron and pulled him bodily off the floor and across the bar, where he hit the floor at O'Brien's feet, bruised and dazed. Before he could react to that, O'Brien kicked him hard in the side, fracturing a rib. The barman yelled out in pain 'Oh, my God!' Gasping it out.

Suddenly the entire room was fixed on the new action. One elderly man shook his head. 'I never seen that before.'

'Get up,' O'Brien growled.

'I can't.' His eyes squinted up.

O'Brien pointed the rifle at him. 'I said, get up.' It took a minute, but the other man managed it.

'Now go back there and read that list of drinks out,' O'Brien commanded him.

'Please.'

'You want me to ask again?' O'Brien suggested casually.

The bartender staggered to the rear wall, holding on to the bar most of the way. Then, breathlessly, he read the short list aloud.

The room was still deathly quiet.

'I'll take the Red Top Rye,' O'Brien called to him. There was some quiet laughter from a couple of tables.

It took the dishevelled barkeep another several minutes to serve O'Brien, watching him warily every moment and holding his side. There was a resumption of quiet talking in the room.

O'Brien swigged the whiskey in one long gulp, while the injured barkeep watched him, holding his breath.

'Now,' O'Brien said. 'That ain't why I come in here. I want to know if any of the Guthrie gang has been in here in the last couple of days.'

The barman spoke through a paper-dry mouth. 'I wouldn't know any of them if I saw them. Honest to God.'

O'Brien studied his face, and believed him. 'All right. Where did that stage robbery take place? Was it near here?'

Sweat had popped out on the other man's forehead. He swallowed hard. 'It was west of here. But that's all I know.' Watching O'Brien's face closely.

'I know where, mister,' a voice came from behind the hunter. O'Brien turned to him.

'It was out west of Scottville. The new agent at the depot told me.'

'How far west?'

'I think he said about three miles. Right where there's a high boulder on the south side of the trail.' He was a townsman, wearing a suit and tie, and was sitting with two other men who looked similar.

111

'Much obliged,' O'Brien said, in a more moderate voice. 'That could help a lot.' He threw some coins on to the bar. 'That's for the Red Top. And for whatever them boys want over there.'

The fellow nodded, still squinting in pain. 'Yes, sir.'

'Thanks, mister.' From the table. 'And for what you did. He's been needing that for some time.'

O'Brien didn't respond. On the way out he busted three louvers in the swinging doors as he pushed through them.

'My God!' from the elderly man. 'Who the hell was that?'

The man at the table again, smiling: 'Somebody you probably don't want to know.'

EIGHT

It was about two hours later when O'Brien found himself out on the stage trail beyond Scottville. He had stopped briefly in that larger town to ask about Guthrie, without success. His face and chest were healing, and he had removed the dressing on his hand at Birney Pass.

He reined in now on the trail, with the landmark boulder just off to the left of the road. Below his mount's feet was a large disturbance in the sandy surface. Of skidding wheel marks and many hoofprints.

O'Brien had been tracking animals and men for three decades, from the time he was a boy in the Shenandoah. He had befriended Iroquois there, and traded with them, usually in partnership with his father. He had learned to hunt and shoot from that Highlander Scot parent, but had absorbed most of his tracking ability from the Iroquois, and later the Sioux.

He dismounted and studied the ground. It was a mess. It hadn't rained here since the robbery, so the ground looked much like it had when that traumatic

113

episode happened for the Wells Fargo men and the unfortunate passengers. The ground told such a vivid story, it was almost like it was all happening again for O'Brien. The air around him crackled with the residue of raw terror and violence.

He walked around the edges of the dusty disturbances, not wanting to contaminate the evidence with his own boots. He walked in circles around the spot, and stopped and ran a hand through his dark mustache. Thinking. Analyzing. He got down on one knee, and looked at individual hoofprints. Yes, there had been four riders. There were also human footprints beside the wheel marks. And then a couple of them looking like they had gotten back in the coach. There were also two places in the sand where bodies had hit the ground.

Over away from that dramatic portrayal, another body had been dragged to the big boulder. O'Brien followed the track over there and found Simon Tate's smelly remains behind the boulder, with blowflies on its eyes. Turkey vultures had been at his face and torso.

'Jesus,' O'Brien muttered.

He went back out to the trail, and studied the ground some more. Yes, there were tracks leading away from the site, and they were of three horses, instead of four. The tracks were headed in a southeasterly direction.

O'Brien thought about that. There were a couple of old trappers' cabins located in that direction. Guthrie could be holed up with his people in one of them.

He had learned a lot.

He walked over to the stallion, which was waiting patiently for him. It nickered quietly when he took the reins.

'I know. You want to get moving. You wonder what's coming up next. So do I.'

First he had to find them. Then he had to figure out what to do about it. Going up against three experienced guns at one time could be fatal. But he would, if he had to. Guthrie had to be dealt with.

He mounted, but did not ride out southeast. He headed back to Scottville to ask a few more questions at the saloons there.

***

Every day that passed at Birney Pass seemed like a week to Sarah. She was a few days past when the doctor thought she would deliver. Olivia Avery was seeing her every day, looking at and listening to Sarah's watermelon belly. On that warm afternoon when O'Brien was returning to Scottville, Olivia was with Sarah in her bedroom. Sarah was partially nude on the bed, with Olivia bending over her, her ear up against Sarah's belly.

'He's a noisy little fellow,' Olivia was smiling. 'But I think he still needs some encouragement.'

In the past couple of days Olivia had been gently manipulating Sarah's belly, pushing in the area where she figured the child's head was, to try to reposition the baby so it would deliver without trouble. The doctor told her it was wasted effort, and that it could even cause Sarah more difficulty when the time came. But Olivia had her own ideas about pregnancy, and continued without the doctor's approval or knowledge.

'You know what, I think we're doing something here,' she reported as she pushed softly on Sarah, almost down to her bare thighs. 'It feels different in there, sweetheart.'

Lovely Sarah looked up at her and smiled. 'I appreciate the effort, Olivia. I just wish it would happen.'

'It will. You just have to get your mind on something else, girl. And I'm predicting a healthy baby boy.' She touched Sarah's cheek.

'I need that. Thanks.'

'The doctor will see you again tomorrow. He thinks he has something that will help make it happen.'

Sarah shook her head. 'I don't want that. I want it all to be natural.'

'You don't have to do anything you don't want to,' Olivia said.

'I just wish O'Brien were here,' Sarah admitted.

Olivia smiled, and pushed back a wisp of gray hair. 'I don't think men are any good at this, dear. He would probably be a nervous wreck by now.'

Sarah laughed quietly. 'I don't think my husband is capable of nervousness.'

Olivia rose, in preparation for leaving. 'I understand he went out after them robbers all by himself.'

Sarah nodded soberly. 'That's the way he is. To stop him, you'd have to hire six strong men to tie him down.'

'But Dru says he's good with that rifle.'

Sarah looked past her. 'Maybe we'd better not talk about it.'

Just then a light knocking came at the bedroom door, and Ethan Purvis's voice came to them. 'It's Ethan, ladies. I got something here Sarah will want to see. Should I come back?'

'Just a minute,' Olivia called back. She pulled a sheet up to cover Sarah.

'All right, come on in.'

Purvis came in looking embarrassed. 'Didn't want to interrupt anything.'

'It's all right, Ethan,' Sarah told him. 'We had just finished up. What is it?'

He walked over to the bed and showed her a paper. 'This is a wire come for you at the local office. I figured you might want to see it right away.'

Sarah frowned curiously. 'A telegram? Where from?'

'It's from that little backwater you two come from. Down in the Indian Territory. From somebody named Pritchard.'

Sarah's face brightened. 'Oh, goodness! Abigail! We both worked for Mayor Spencer!'

'I'll just excuse myself,' Olivia announced, giving Sarah a last smile. Then she left the room.

Purvis handed Sarah the wire. 'I kind of looked at it before I knew what it was,' he said apologetically. 'I told Dru about it. She'll be right in.'

'Thanks, Ethan.'

He left just as she began reading the telegram.

GREETINGS FROM THE BACK OF BEYOND. THE MAYOR SENDS HIS BEST. ALL WELL WITH ME, BUT MISS YOU. SORRY TO REPORT THIS. MR. SMITH HAS PASSED. SOMETHING WITH HIS HEART. EXPRESS NOW RUN BY OUTSIDERS. OTHERWISE ALL FINE. HOPE ALL WELL WITH YOU AND THAT WILD MAN. LOVE.

Sarah dropped the paper heavily to her lap, her eyes already moistening. 'Oh, dear. Smitty. Oh, my God.'

Dru walked in at that moment and saw Sarah's reaction. She went and sat on the edge of the bed, and laid a hand on Sarah's shoulder. 'Ethan told me. He read it. Was he a good friend?'

Sarah wiped at an eye. With Smitty gone, those days in the Territory really were a thing of the now-dead past. She had become a Colorado girl, embroiled in a whole new existence. One she hoped had some permanency.

'The very best,' she finally responded. Then her face changed. 'Oh, God! O'Brien!'

'He knows, honey. Ethan just told me. He just didn't want to upset you at this time.'

'They went back decades together. Went through life-or-death times on the trail. It must be awful for him.'

'He seems to be handling it well,' Dru assured her. 'He's more concerned about you. And Guthrie. But

I'm sorry, love. Are you about ready to let that boy out of there?'

Sarah wiped at an eye, and tried a smile. 'I was ready when I got here.'

Dru's face went somber. 'Ethan is leaving tomorrow. Taking that no-account deputy with him. Heading for Culver Junction and Scottville. I think he's hoping to get some help from the town marshals. For Guthrie.' She looked down. 'I don't know whether I'm supposed to tell you this. But now that you know about Smith, I guess it's all right.'

'What, Dru?'

'Just before O'Brien rode off, he told Ethan something. It seems that Guthrie's name jogged a memory from a few years back, and it came to him just when he was here with us in town. I guess Smith had told O'Brien back then that a man named Guthrie had shot and killed a cousin of his in a saloon fight, down in Texas, and Smith always regretted that he was unable to answer that. O'Brien thinks this is the same man, from the description. So maybe you and the cabin aren't the only reasons he thinks Guthrie is his personal responsibility. He probably thinks he owes his old friend this. Especially now.'

Sarah lay there propped on her pillow, looking past Dru. 'Yes.' Thoughtfully. 'Of course.'

Dru sighed. 'I just thought that might make you feel a little better. About him going off by himself like that.'

Sarah nodded. 'Yes. It does. Thanks, Dru.'

A moment later Dru was gone, and Sarah lay there with her green eyes damp. 'Please,' she choked out. 'Come back to us.'

***

It had been a fairly brief ride into Scottville for O'Brien. The main street was busy with wagons and carriages. It was a bigger town than either Birney Pass or Culver Junction. When O'Brien had stopped there briefly before, he had gotten nothing about the gang in two saloons where he had inquired. This time he stopped at the town marshal's office at the end of a dusty street and went inside.

There was a young man sitting behind an old desk that was littered with paper: warrants, civic announcements, 'Wanted' posters. One of the latter had Guthrie's name on it, and a rough drawing of his face.

The young man looked up at O'Brien with little interest. 'Mister, can I help you?' Looking O'Brien over with a light frown. 'Are you the marshal?' O'Brien asked with incredulity.

The fellow got the tone of the question, and the frown deepened. 'No, he's not here. But I can do anything he can.'

O'Brien reached to the desk and picked up the dodger on Guthrie, and studied it.

'Hey! You can't have that!' Rising from the desk.

'Where is he?' O'Brien pursued, not looking up at him.

'He's down at the saloon, if it's any of your business!'

120

O'Brien laid the poster back down on the desk, as the young fellow glanced warily at the Winchester under O'Brien's right arm.

'Are you his deputy?'

'Damn right!'

'Are you even out of school?' O'Brien said caustically.

The deputy's face colored. 'You're talking to an officer of the law, rawhide man. You ain't out in the mountains now. You should show some respect!'

'I'll show some when it's needed,' O'Brien replied quietly. 'In the meantime, maybe you ought to play it down a little. You might live longer.'

Before the deputy could think of a response, O'Brien was gone.

It was a short walk down the street with the stallion to the nearest of two saloons, where O'Brien expected the marshal would walk to. It was called The Water Trough, and despite the name, it had a higher class look than the one in Culver Junction.

O'Brien hitched his mount outside, climbed three steps to a doorway and pushed through. Inside there was a long mahogany bar, polished and clean-looking, and a number of patrons already enjoying the establishment's fare, at tables and standing at the bar. There were men playing cards at a faro table at the rear, and a closed-up piano.

O'Brien walked over to an obese bartender. 'A black ale,' he ordered.

The fellow wiped at the bar with a towel. 'Coming up. You get a boiled egg with that if you want it.'

'I'll pass,' O'Brien told him.

A moment later the ale was there and O'Brien swigged part of it. 'I was told I might find the marshal in here,' he said then to the bartender. He had laid the rifle on the bar, and the bartender was eyeing it now.

'He's here. That boy at the center table over there, sitting with another man.' O'Brien turned and saw the two men pointed out. 'Much obliged.'

He picked up his ale glass and walked over to the table, the rifle under his arm again. When the two men saw him coming, they stopped talking. 'Marshal Davison?' O'Brien asked, addressing the man with a star on his vest.

'The same,' Davison replied, looking O'Brien over and noticing the primitive look of him. 'You got business with me, mister?'

O'Brien nodded. 'Can I sit a minute?'

Davison smiled. 'Our pleasure. Rest your freight.'

O'Brien sat down, and leaned the Winchester against the table. 'You carry heavy iron,' the marshal commented.

'It's all I know,' O'Brien offered.

Both the marshal and his companion grinned at that. 'This is an old friend from Culver Junction,' Davison said, 'name of Foley.'

O'Brien nodded. 'How can I help you?'

The marshal was a thick-set man with silver hair under a dark brown Stetson, and bigger than his companion.

'You know all about a rattlesnake that calls himself Wade Guthrie, I guess.'

Their faces both changed. 'Who hasn't?' the marshal replied. 'If that weasel don't go to hell, we might as well not have one.'

'He's got the whole town of Culver Junction on edge,' Foley added. 'We haven't seen nothing like this.'

'Have you made any effort to locate him?' O'Brien asked.

'I've asked some questions. But he hasn't done anything here. He's the county's responsibility.'

O'Brien gave him a look. 'Well, I'm going after him.' Davison frowned. 'You been deputized?'

A shake of the head. 'It's personal.' Davison studied that square face. 'I see.'

'You probably don't,' O'Brien countered. 'But I'm hoping you can help me.'

The marshal sighed. 'You better give this a second thought, Mister...'

'Call me O'Brien.'

'All right, O'Brien. But I don't know much. We think he's responsible for both Wells Fargo robberies, and that he's hiding out here in the county.'

'I saw tracks heading south from the stage hold-up. I think there's a cabin or two down in that direction. Do you know if anybody has checked down there?'

'I doubt it. It sure wouldn't be this office. Have you gone to Sheriff Purvis?'

'He hasn't been there either,' O'Brien grunted out.

'I know of one down there. It's not a long ride from here. Sits close to Willow Creek. I think a trapper built it. That might be a good place to look, come to think of it.'

'I might check it out,' O'Brien said.

Davison studied that resolute face again. 'Look. I could ride along if you're determined about this. But I'd have no real jurisdiction.'

O'Brien gave a half-grin. 'I'm good with alone. And I don't need no jurisdiction.'

Davison returned the grin. 'You seem like a very determined man.'

O'Brien grunted. 'Guthrie made me that way.'

It was obvious he wasn't interested in discussing it. 'Is there any other way I can help?' Davison asked.

'Well, I understand there's three of them now. Since that little one got it at the last hold-up.'

'That's right. His name was Tate – they were all seen in saloons and stores before they started their rampage. Now it's just Guthrie and that half-breed, and a new boy we haven't identified.'

'What do they look like?' O'Brien asked.

'Guthrie looks like a banker. Dresses neat. We got a dodger on him.'

'I saw it,' O'Brien said.

'Not a bad-looking fellow. You'd probably sit and drink with him if you didn't know him. Anyway, that's what I hear. I haven't met him. He was cashiered out of the Texas Rangers for unnecessary killing. He's tall, about your height, and has a badly broken nose. Somebody I talked to says he reads. Owns books. The Rangers say he's a cold-blooded killer, and I think he's proved that here.'

'What about the other two?'

'The new man was seen with him in a saloon. Almost as tall as Guthrie. Dark hair. Slim. Carries two Colt Army .45s.'

'And the half-breed?'

'A boy with a strange name. Calls himself Skin Walker. He's part Lakota. Slim, hard. You'll recognize him, he wears his hair in a braid at the back. He's lightning fast with his gun.'

O'Brien nodded. 'I know about the name. Early tribes used to take enemies alive and skin them and dance around in their skin. They figured it was powerful medicine.'

'He sounds like he don't have it all up here,' Davison said, pointing to his head.

'That might describe all of them,' O'Brien commented. He rose from his chair. 'You been a big help, Marshal. Pleasured to meet up with you, Foley. Now I got trail to ride.'

'Be careful down there,' Davison advised. O'Brien nodded, and was gone.

O'Brien made two stops before leaving town that afternoon. He went into a small restaurant down the street and had his only real meal of the day, a bowl of beef stew, and then stopped at a gun store a few doors farther down. When he got inside, he jarred the clerk there by laying the big Winchester on the counter.

'Yes, sir.' With wary eyes. 'What can I do for you?'

'The lever action on this gun is getting a little play in it. Can you snug it up while I wait?'

The clerk nodded. 'I can do that.' He picked the Winchester up and admired it. 'Going hunting?'

O'Brien gave him a look. 'Just get at it.'

A sober nod. He levered the rifle, which O'Brien had emptied. 'Hey. This action feels pretty good. You sure you want to spend the money? I can sell you a nice little Derringer instead.'

'Pretty good ain't good enough,' O'Brien said irritably. 'Like I said, do it. I want to be on my way. And do it right.'

Another nod. 'Sure. Whatever you say.'

Just at that moment another customer walked into the store.

He was a mountain of a man, a couple of inches taller than O'Brien and weighing close to three hundred pounds, thick around the waist.

'Henry,' he boomed out at the clerk.

'Oh, Big John. Nice to see you again.'

Big John ignored O'Brien, and placed hams of hands on the counter. 'I need a couple boxes of them eight-gauges you sold me before,' he went on. 'I'm going after grouse tomorrow.'

'Sure,' Henry replied. 'I'll take care of you soon as I adjust the lever on a rifle for this gentleman.'

John glanced at O'Brien finally. 'No, I ain't waiting around here while you fiddle around with no rifle, Henry. You just go get them shells and I'll get out of here.'

Henry looked over at O'Brien nervously.

'You heard me. I'm in a hurry,' O'Brien told him. 'Get on with that adjustment.'

Henry looked from O'Brien to Big John.

'The ammo will take some looking for, John, and this boy was ahead of you.' Timidly.

Now the big man really turned to O'Brien for the first time. 'I ain't never seen you before. You from around here?' He was wearing work clothes and an enormous soiled vest over them.

'No,' O'Brien said impatiently.

John turned back to Henry. 'Well, goddam it, you think you're going to serve some buckskin stranger over a regular local?'

'Well, if you really need them,' Henry said tightly, looking at O'Brien again. 'Maybe I could look for you.'

'You screw around with that rifle first, and I'll come back there and ram it up your behind!' John added.

O'Brien met the clerk's eyes. 'I think you heard me. I want that Winchester worked on now.'

Henry just stood there, his hands shaking now. Big John muttered something under his breath and stormed over to O'Brien. He didn't say a word when he got there, but hauled off and threw a fist at O'Brien that could have gone through a wall. O'Brien was caught by surprise, but threw a hand up, his healing one, and partially deflected the blow, which still caught him on the side of his face, almost breaking his jaw.

O'Brien fell against the counter, and almost went down. 'Sonofabitch!' he muttered. His lower lip was also bleeding. John, surprised O'Brien was still standing, moved in to throw a second blow. He swung

127

rather wildly, and this time O'Brien ducked to one side and threw a fist into the thick waist as John stumbled past. The big man exhaled a gush of air as he doubled over, trying to keep his feet. O'Brien moved around in front of him as he tried to come up, and threw a sledgehammer blow at the centre of John's meaty face. There were loud cracking sounds as his nose, jaw and teeth fractured, sending him flying across the room. When he hit the floor on his back, it made the whole building shake. A leg twitched, but otherwise there was no movement. Front teeth were scattered on the floor near him, and there was a lot of blood on his lower face and vest.

Henry had watched tensely through all of that. He looked warily at O'Brien now. Breathlessly, he said, 'Holy Mary. I didn't think anybody could do that!'

O'Brien looked over at him, rubbing his fist. 'Why the hell are you still standing there?'

NINE

Ethan Purvis slumped on his parlor sofa, looking glum and bitter. On his left leg was a cast that ran from his hip to his ankle. Dru sat on a chair facing him, concern on her face. He had left town that morning with his deputy, not long after O'Brien's departure, to go looking for information on Guthrie. He had been back by noon, being held on his saddle by the deputy.

They had surprised a cougar in rocky terrain, and Purvis' horse had reared and thrown him off, where he had hit the rock-strewn ground hard and broken his leg. The doctor had just reset the leg and applied the cast, and was now in with Sarah.

'Damn blind luck!' he grumbled, pounding his fist on the sofa. 'I wish I'd shot that devil cat!'

Dru sighed. 'I'm real sorry, Ethan.' It was the fourth time she had expressed her sympathy.

'The doc says this will lay me up for weeks!' He looked down with disgust at the cast. 'I had some ideas. There's a cabin down south that I wanted to check out. If there's somebody living there they

129

might know something about Guthrie. I'd hoped to run into O'Brien, and maybe he'd change his mind about taking my help. Now all that's gone. O'Brien is on his own.

'Well, that's the way he wanted it...'

Purvis eyed her somberly. 'His head ain't directing him, Dru. He's got a fire in his belly that could get him killed. He's going up against three dangerous guns. I have no idea how he intends to handle it.'

Dru sighed again. 'Maybe he does, Ethan. Let's have a little faith in him. And don't let Sarah see your long face. She has enough on her pretty head. She started having contractions while you were gone, but they come and go.'

'That don't sound good.'

'We'll see. I sent for Olivia. The doctor can't set up shop here. But it looks like this will happen in the next day or two.' She paused. 'I like her, Ethan. I don't want anything to happen to her.'

Purvis suddenly felt insensitive complaining about his leg. 'Oh hell, Dru. I ain't hardly spoke to her since I got back, and she was so concerned about me, for God's sake. Is that little sweetheart in trouble?'

'I don't know yet. I don't think the doctor knows. We just have to wait and see. She looked towards a closed bedroom door.

On the other side of that door, the doctor was bending over Sarah again and listening to her bare belly through a stethoscope. She was half propped on a pillow, mild distress showing in her green eyes.

The doctor straightened up and pulled a sheet up to her waist, where she was clothed in a peignoir bought from Boston. 'When was your last contraction?' he asked her.

'Almost three hours ago,' she told him.

He frowned.

'Is this really going to happen, Doctor?' she asked soberly. 'I'm beginning to wonder.'

He smiled. 'Oh, it will happen, all right. It's just how it will happen we don't know yet.' He paused. 'Are you sure you don't want to try this new pill I have that's supposed to encourage the process? There's no evidence yet that it can hurt you in any way.'

'They told my mother that in Boston, just before a new procedure ended her life,' Sarah countered.

'Oh. I'm sorry.'

'Olivia thinks it will all work out without that,' she added. 'And I tend to agree with her.'

He regarded her seriously. 'Olivia is a fine woman. She's assisted me in a lot of deliveries. But she's not a doctor, dear.'

Sarah sighed. She wished O'Brien were there. She valued his judgment over everybody else's. And he was always so positive about everything, so sure everything would come out all right. And she had this completely illogical conviction deep inside her that nothing really bad could happen to her if he was with her.

'Let's see how it goes,' she finally told him.

When he was gone, Sarah wanted to get out of bed and join Dru and Ethan in the parlor, but she realized she no longer had the strength for such activity. And she had no sooner rejected that idea when a sharp pain grabbed her down there, followed by a second, lesser one. She made a face, and then was breathing more shallowly. There was nothing more.

She looked down at her covered belly with a frown. 'Come on out of there, you stubborn little O'Brien!' Then, more quietly, 'Sorry.'

At that moment Dru came into the room. A look of quiet concern on her face. 'What did the doctor say, honey?'

'Not much,' Sarah said. 'How is Ethan doing with that cast?'

'Oh, you know men. If he can't mount a horse he thinks his world has fallen apart. I don't think he's having much pain. The doctor gave him some laudanum.'

'That will help him,' Sarah said.

'He said he'll try to hobble in here to look in on you directly.'

'Tell him to stay put. Neither of us is ambulatory. I just wish I had one of my books to read. Jane Austen would cheer me up.'

'Who?'

Sarah smiled. 'She was probably the world's finest writer. Died earlier this century. I would have lent her to you.'

'I don't read much,' Dru admitted. 'But I hear they might build a library right here in Birney Pass one of these days soon. You'd like that, I guess.'

'It would be wonderful.'

Dru hesitated before she continued. 'Do you like living way out in the boonies like you been doing, honey?

Sarah shrugged. 'O'Brien likes it.'

'That isn't what I asked.'

Sarah frowned. 'Well, sure. I like it. I like my husband to be happy with his life. He tried town living, down in Fort Revenge. He didn't like it very much. He's lived all his life in open country. Sleeping on the ground. Eating out of tins. He's just now adapting to domestication. Weeding tomatoes. Sleeping in a real bed with me.'

'That must be the best part of it,' Dru grinned.

Sarah smiled. 'But at least he still spends most of his time trapping. If he didn't have that, it would hurt him.'

'If he lived in town here, he could still do that.'

Sarah frowned at her.

'Ethan says a house come up for sale down at the end of town. A two-storey place with three bedrooms. Plenty of space for a family. The place needs some work, but that would be easier than re-building that cabin from the ground up.'

'You think we should move into town?' Sarah said.

'Until this area gets safer for settlers, you and the baby would be better off here. You'll need all kinds of stuff now you didn't before, and we got a nice general store here. Life would be more convenient. Ethan said he's sure you could meet the asking price.'

The idea was completely foreign to Sarah. 'Well, I guess it would be fine with me. So O'Brien wouldn't have to do all that work over again. But you're talking to the wrong person, Dru.'

'I couldn't talk to that hunter of yours. He scares me a little.'

Sarah laughed lightly. 'He scared me when I first met him. But you haven't seen how good he can be with people when he knows them and likes them.'

'I'm sure,' Dru said doubtfully.

'And of course,' Sarah added, 'at the moment, where we live might be the least important issue each of us faces.'

Dru nodded apologetically. 'Forget I mentioned it, Sarah. I was just trying to get your mind off all this.'

Sarah gave her a weary look. 'I guess it didn't work,' she smiled at her friend.

***

At the cabin hideaway of Wade Guthrie, he and his reduced gang sat at the table that occupied the center of the room, drinking from a tall whiskey bottle and discussing the immediate future. Brett St Clair, slim and suave-looking, sat back relaxed on his chair, with no vest and a dark shirt unbuttoned partway down his chest.

'I'm just thinking how to spend all that money you made for us,' he grinned at Guthrie, 'I might skip Mexico and head for California later. Open up a gaming hall. I hear people have a lot of cash to spend out there.'

Guthrie just sat there silently.

'I already have it figured out what I will do,' Skin Walker said thoughtfully, in his Lakota accent. 'I will take my money to a little tribe where I know the chief, and spread it around a little, and buy myself a position as medicine man. Dance around a fire now and then. Say some prayers to the coyote god. Shake some badger bones. I could end up making goddam laws, you know? Running the show. Be more powerful than the territorial governor!'

Guthrie shook his head solemnly. 'Wealth and fame are fleeting, boys. Didn't you know that?' He was feeling the alcohol, as he continued:

'The worldly hope men set their hearts upon
Turns ashes... or it prospers; and anon,
Like snow upon the desert's dusty face,
Lighting a little hour or two... is gone.'

St Clair cast a serious frown at him, studying his face.

'Hey! I know that one!' from Walker. 'That eastern boy. Edgar Allen something, ain't it?'

'You are a literary moron, Indian,' Guthrie commented, swigging the remains of whiskey from his glass. 'Just right for a medicine man.'

St Clair sat there wondering about Guthrie. There was less doubt in his mind as the days passed. After their next job, he would part company again with Guthrie and go out on his own. And leave Guthrie to his dark philosophies and abject disregard for his fellow men.

'Have you decided on what bank you want to take first?' he asked Guthrie then.

135

Guthrie nodded. 'There's a sweet little one over at Smith's Ford, west of Scottville. We'll make a visit there first, to check it out. But a baby could open the safe. And they can't afford guards. It's perfect. Two or three like that and we can all retire. Anywhere we want.'

St Clair didn't mention he wouldn't be doing two or three more.

'When do you figure on taking it?'

Guthrie sat forward on his chair. 'Within the week. But we have to move out of this cabin.'

They both looked curiously at him.

'Move out?' Walker frowned.

'That dumb wild man will come after me now.'

'O'Brien?' St Clair wondered. He had been told about Morgan and Garrett, and the burning of the cabin.

Guthrie nodded. 'He's just stupid enough to come on his own. But that Birney Pass sheriff might persuade him to accept his help. In other words, I don't know how many will be looking for us. But that goddam trapper will be one of them. And I hear he's pretty damn good with that rifle. I don't want him getting lucky and messing things up for us. So I'm going to make it harder for him to find us. Somebody might have seen us out here. We're moving. There's another unoccupied cabin down south and west of here, hidden in aspens. At least I think it's still unoccupied. We'll have an evening meal here, then St Clair and me will ride down there.'

'What about me?' Walker frowned.

RETURN OF THE BUFFALO HUNTER

'Somebody has to stay here to watch our goods while we check. If we're not back here tomorrow, you'll pack up a few things and bring them on down there with you. I'll tell you what before we leave, as well as the directions to the cabin.'

St Clair was frowning. 'All that seems unnecessary, Wade.' He intended to be gone after the bank. 'If somebody finds us here, we'll handle it. Get it over with.'

Suddenly Guthrie was on his feet, feeling the liquor in him. His face had clouded over. 'Have you decided you want to run this show, Brett? Would you like to challenge for leadership?' Fiercely.

St Clair's frown deepened. 'For Christ's sake, Wade. Of course not.'

'Because if you have ideas of taking my place, I by God want to know it!' Slightly red-faced.

St Clair was stunned. He hadn't seen Guthrie yet with liquor in him. 'You know better than that. We both know you're calling the shots. That's the way we want it. I was just making a suggestion.'

Guthrie sat back down, slowly. 'Well, here's the way it is. When I tell you I want to do something, I don't want any goddam suggestions. We do things my way, or you ride.' He paused. 'If that's feasible.' In a warning voice.

Neither St Clair nor Walker responded to that outburst.

Guthrie looked away, calming. 'Damn it, I'm under a lot of pressure here. Making decisions for us.' He already wished he hadn't burned O'Brien's cabin.

137

'I haven't had this situation before. Where I have to deal with some loony besides the incompetent law. It adds an unpredictable factor, and I don't like unpredictability.'

'I can appreciate that,' St Clair said quietly, casting a private look at Walker.

Walker decided to help out. 'Maybe I can make it all a little more predictable.'

They both looked over at him. He was bareheaded, and looked very Indian, with his black hair braided behind his head. He was wearing only a vest at the moment, with no shirt, and there was a Lakota bracelet on his upper arm.

'After you leave later, I could ride into Culver Junction or Scottville and ask around to find out if there's anybody in the area looking for us. And who it might be.'

Guthrie thought that over. Ordinarily he wouldn't want Walker in town until after the bank job. But he was becoming tight inside about who might be coming for him.

'Not a bad idea,' he admitted grudgingly. 'Go to Culver Junction first. If you get nothing, you can ride on over to Scottville before you return here.'

Walker was grinning because Guthrie had accepted an idea of his, which was rare. 'I know the bartender at Culver Junction.' He was referring to the man O'Brien had had trouble with earlier. 'I think he likes me.' Searching Guthrie's face for approval, and then that of St Clair.

'All right, all right,' Guthrie muttered. 'Just use your head. Keep away from the law.'

'I have this gut feeling,' Walker said.

'What gut feeling?' Guthrie growled.

'I feel the hunter. Like he's close by somewhere. I feel it right here, in my belly. We have this sixth sense, you know.'

Guthrie shook his head. 'Fine. If you run on to him, kill him.'

Walker nodded. 'I'll shake some bones.'

***

O'Brien rode up to the cabin hideout in early evening, and reined in fifty yards away, studying it and its surroundings. The first thing that caught his attention was that there were no horses anywhere in sight. But there was still a light wisp of smoke rising from a stone chimney. His brow furrowed. Maybe this was the wrong place.

He picketed the stallion to a nearby cottonwood sapling, slid the big Winchester from its saddle scabbard, and moved carefully up a gentle slope to the cabin, keeping a watch around him. He could see things other men couldn't, and according to Shanghai Smith, could hear a sidearm being drawn from a holster in a windstorm.

He was at the cabin. There were no windows to reveal to him what was inside. He listened at the thick door, and heard nothing.

139

He made a decision. He stepped back, raised a booted foot, and kicked the door inward with a loud crash, stepping inside with the rifle ready.

There was no one there.

O'Brien stood there for a moment, looking around. A table and chairs. Bunks and cots. A smoldering fireplace that had been burning recently. Then he spotted a small shelf holding several books, and knew he was in the right place. Guthrie was known to be a reader.

He swore softly under his breath. They were gone off somewhere. Guthrie wouldn't leave his books behind, so they would probably return here. But there was no way of knowing when. It could be days. Or possibly never.

He had a strong urge to destroy the books, as Guthrie had destroyed those of Sarah. But that would tell them he had been here. The door he had kicked open was unharmed, and he had left no other evidence.

He went back outside, closing the door carefully behind him. Dusk had fallen, and there was a small symphony of crickets and cicadas. A half-moon hung over his head. He walked to the side of the cabin where the mounts had been tethered, and saw the hoofprints, the same ones he had seen at the stage hold-up site. Most of them headed off in a southerly direction but quickly disappeared over rocky ground. A last set started out north, toward Culver Junction, and was easier to read. He decided to ride north.

It was dark when he rode into Culver Junction. It was a small town, and looked very quiet at this time.

He rode down to the Culver Pass saloon, where he had had trouble with the bartender earlier in the day, which was beginning to seem like a week ago now. There was a lot of noise coming from inside, as usual in the evening.

If one of them had ridden here, he might be in the saloon. So O'Brien dismounted, tethered the big horse to a hitching rail, and went inside, taking the rifle with him.

O'Brien had guessed right. Walker had preceded him there, to inquire about any gathering of law in the area. He knew the bartender personally from previous visits, and directed his attention to that tough-looking fellow. His name was Gus, and he had a tape on his ribs where O'Brien had busted one after dragging Gus over the bar to get his attention. Gus said he had seen no law, but some crazy hunter had come nosing around.

A clammy hand had grabbed at Walker's insides with that report, because he knew exactly who the hunter was.

Now, just before O'Brien pushed through the swinging doors, Gus had taken Walker to a store room through a door at the back of the room, to show him a crate of imported Cuban rum he had just purchased, and they were still there when O'Brien entered.

O'Brien scanned the noisy room carefully, but did not see anyone who fitted the descriptions he had of the outlaws. He walked over to the bar and saw that the bartender who had given him the trouble wasn't there.

'Anybody working here tonight?' he growled at another drinker down the bar a short distance.

'He's out in back,' the man replied. 'He'll be right back, I reckon.'

O'Brien was in a bad mood. He swore under his breath again, and went and sat at a table nearby, facing the front entrance. Hoping one of them might still show up.

He had no idea how he would proceed next if that didn't happen. He knew only that he would keep after Guthrie until he found him. He had just finished that thought when Gus came back into the room alone. He had left Walker out the back to look over some inventory he might want to buy. Gus saw O'Brien as soon as he got behind the bar.

'Oh, Jesus,' he muttered. But he had no idea that O'Brien's presence would be significant to Walker. Walker had kept that to himself. Reluctantly he went to O'Brien's table. 'You again.' Grimly.

O'Brien eyed him acidly. 'You only work part-time now? Bring me a black ale, and if you water it, I'll know it.'

'We got the best ale in the county,' Gus replied quietly, remembering the fractured rib. 'It will just be a minute.'

As the bartender was returning to the bar, Skin Walker emerged from the store room carrying a tall bottle of rum. But he had taken just three steps into the room when he saw O'Brien's broad back at the center table, and knew immediately who it was.

142

Nobody had noticed him come in, or saw the sudden look of raw emotion crowd on to his face. O'Brien was still watching the front door and had just received his ale, his back to Walker.

Walker felt several emotions course through him in rapid succession. The dominant one was fear. But then, as he carefully set the bottle on the end of the bar, and got himself under control, he realized what had happened. He had shaken the bones, and he had prayed. And the coyote god had intervened to give him this incredible opportunity.

O'Brien was now drinking his ale, and making plans for later, when Walker walked up behind him and spoke to him above the other noise.

'Keep your hands away from that long gun.'

O'Brien frowned, and then understood. 'Sonofabitch,' he muttered.

'I'm aimed at the back of your head. And I can't miss.' A hard smile.

O'Brien knew it was too late to go for the Winchester. And it was his only weapon, except for the skinning knife in the sheath on his right stove-pipe boot. He sighed heavily and decided to keep his assailant talking. He noticed that all noise had subsided in the room around them suddenly. Gus had seen the action, and a big grin etched itself on to his face.

'Well, well,' he purred with satisfaction.

'You must be the Indian,' O'Brien said, from the sound of the voice.

'That's right, buffalo man,' Walker replied, breath-lessly. 'And I wanted you to know I'm the one that killed the White Lakota.'

'I'd like to face you when you do it,' O'Brien said in Lakota.

Walker hesitated, then responded in the same language. 'If that's the way you want it. I never seen your face, anyway.'

The new silence in the room was tomb-like. Gus watched happily from behind the bar. O'Brien rose and turned, the rifle still on the table, and when Walker saw the calm, deadly look in his eyes, he had a moment of doubt. He re-aimed carefully. 'It's over, Thunderbird man. I shook the bones. Have a good trip.' His finger whitened on the trigger.

O'Brien, though, had gotten up with the ale glass in his left hand. And just before the gun fired, he threw the glass of dark liquid into Walker's surprised face, just a few feet away.

Walker squinted and sputtered for a moment, and the Joslyn fired loudly and hot lead missed O'Brien's left ear by a half-inch and shattered a lamp on the front wall. In the same instant, O'Brien reached to the sheath on his boot and hurled the Bowie with its ten-inch blade at Walker's chest before he could aim again. The knife thumped audibly into Walker's chest, just over his heart, and buried itself there halfway to the hilt.

Walker just stood there for a moment, trying to understand. The Joslyn fired again, into the floor. He looked at O'Brien in perplexity, then started slowly walking toward the front doors. As the entire

144

room watched in fascination, he made it almost there, staggering drunkenly, then collapsed to the floor on to his face, the knife punching all the way through his chest.

O'Brien set the glass down, retrieved the rifle, and walked to the half-breed. He turned him over, pulled the Bowie from his chest, wiped it on Walker's vest, then returned it to its sheath.

He decided he didn't want another ale. He turned to the bartender, who stood with his mouth agape in the silence of the room.

'Bet you had your money on the Indian, didn't you?'

Then he was gone.

TEN

The day after O'Brien's confrontation with Walker, Guthrie and St Clair were settled in at the new cabin. While O'Brien was taking a hotel room for the night in Culver Junction until he could decide on his next move against Guthrie, the two outlaws were cleaning up the new place. It wasn't as good as the one they had vacated, but it had a double bunk, a front and rear door, and two unglazed windows beside them, which Guthrie intended to cover with cloth as soon as Walker arrived with their things.

They had brought some meager supplies with them, and had just finished coffee and biscuits at a rickety table when Guthrie looked through the open front window thoughtfully.

'I'm not waiting another day or two to get our stuff here, like I told the Indian,' he said to St Clair. 'We need those blankets, and grub. And I want my books. I think I'm going to let you ride on back there today while I finish cleaning up here. You and Walker bring everything here. We have to make this habitable for a while.'

St Clair was becoming familiar with Guthrie's impatience. 'Sure, Wade. I can ride back there. We could be back by midday.'

'Be sure to bring all the food we left behind. Clean the place out. And remember I'm waiting back here.'

St Clair nodded and rose. 'I'm gone already.'

A few minutes later St Clair rode off, heading north. It wasn't a long ride, and he arrived at the cabin in mid-morning. The first thing he noticed was that Walker's horse wasn't visible anywhere.

'What the hell,' he said curiously.

He dismounted and entered the cabin, gun drawn. It looked just as they had left it, but no Walker. He took a minute to look around the place. Nothing seemed disturbed. He holstered the gun and just stood there. Walker had been instructed to ride in to Culver Junction to see if a posse was out looking for them. But he should have been back last night. He wondered if the half-breed had gotten drunk there and was sleeping it off in some sleazy hotel.

He had to find out.

St Clair got on his mount again, and headed for Culver Junction. He was there about noon, and went directly to the saloon where Walker knew the bartender.

On this day there was hardly anybody there when he walked in. He scanned the room for badges, but found none. The bartender had just emerged from the same store room where he had taken Walker yesterday. St Clair went over to him.

'Yeah?' Gus welcomed him. 'What's your poison?'

147

'I'm not drinking,' St Clair told him. 'I'm looking for a man you might know. A half-breed named Walker.'

Gus' eyes widened. 'You know him?'

St Clair frowned. 'Where is he?'

The barkeep shook his head. 'Walker is dead, mister.'

The frown deepened. 'Dead? Did the law find him?'

'Oh, no. There ain't been no law in here. It was that wild man again. That hunter.'

St Clair's face changed. He stared past Gus.

'Killed him with a goddam knife. I never seen nothing like it. He's down at the morgue, if you want to see him before they put him under.'

St Clair collected himself. 'Uh. No, but thanks. This hunter... Do you know if he's still in town?'

'Hell, how would I know? I just hope he don't come in here again. No telling what he might do next.'

St Clair nodded, his head swimming. 'Much obliged.'

'Say, I can sell you a nice glass of imported rum to send you on your way!'

But St Clair was on his way out.

Outside, he wondered if he should look for O'Brien in town before he left. Take the offensive, so to speak. He surely could take the hunter in a face-down. That would endear him to Guthrie. But Morgan, Garrett and Walker had probably figured the same thing.

He decided to ride back to Guthrie and endure his new wrath.

He was gone a few minutes later, and by mid-afternoon he was back at the cabin with Guthrie. He sat down at the table with Guthrie before he spoke.

'Well?' Guthrie demanded. 'Why are you here alone? Where is our stuff?'

St Clair took a deep breath. 'Walker is dead. O'Brien killed him.'

Guthrie carefully set a coffee cup down, staring hard at St Clair. 'What the hell are you saying?'

'The hunter found him at that saloon. Killed him with a knife. Probably one of those Bowies they use for skinning.' He watched Guthrie's face, not knowing what he might do.

Guthrie rose slowly, paying no further attention to St Clair. Then he turned, picked up his chair, and hurled it across the room, where it smashed in pieces against a wall. Then he picked up his coffee cup and threw it violently at a pot-belly stove, where it shattered loudly. Then he just stood breathless, his face twisted with rage. But this time, underneath the anger, was also a growing fear.

'We could go after him,' St Clair ventured quietly. 'He might still be in Culver Junction. Or Scottville.'

'Why the hell didn't you do that while you were there?' Guthrie yelled at him red-faced.

St Clair shrugged. 'I figured it would be a more certain take-down if we confronted him together.'

'This sonofabitch is going to spoil this whole thing for us if we let him.'

'He's reduced our numbers. But you and me can take that bank without the breed. Then we can leave the goddam county to the hunter, and do the same thing somewhere else.' But he would be through with Guthrie after that next job, he had already decided that privately.

Guthrie had calmed down. 'Well. That's not a bad idea. I know Texas pretty well, and how to avoid the Rangers. That's something to think about. In the meantime, we're hitting that bank tomorrow.'

'Didn't you want to check it over again first?'

Guthrie scowled at the floor. 'I'm tired of sitting here in this rat-hole of a cabin. I'm tired of wondering if that crazy man will show up some night and surprise us. We're going.'

St Clair grinned. 'I guess we're going.'

***

O'Brien had arrived at the Culver Pass saloon in less than a half-hour after St Clair had ridden out. He had had a good rest in a rare hotel bed and had learned something important from the hotel proprietor. The man told him of a second cabin in the area, south of where O'Brien had been, surrounded by aspens. O'Brien had decided to check it out, since he had no other leads. He had gone to the saloon to make sure Guthrie hadn't come looking for Walker, but had missed St Clair.

By late morning he was on his way to find the cabin.

When he rode past the first cabin, he took the time to check it out again, even though there was no evidence anyone was there. He went inside again, and it looked the same as it had before. A puzzled look came on to his square face. All of their belongings were there, which seemed to mean they were still using it.

He shook his head. What was the point in riding on down to some abandoned cabin when there was no evidence they had ever left this one. He leaned against a wall in there, thinking over what to do. Guthrie's books were still there. There was even food on a shelf. The whole idea of their being in a different hideout seemed illogical now.

But he had nothing else to do. And even if he rode on down there, found nothing and returned, this situation would undoubtedly be the same. Five minutes later he was back on the stallion and riding south.

It took him a while to find the place, but as soon as it was in sight he saw the light smoke coming from a tin chimney. And he heard the quiet nickering of a horse behind the cabin.

'Well,' he growled in his throat.

This had to be them.

He dismounted fifty yards away, hiding his mount in aspens. He removed his riding spurs and left them in a saddlebag. Then he slid the long gun from its scabbard and checked its ammunition.

This was it.

He headed for the cabin.

Unknown to him, though, both outlaws were out at the back of the cabin at that moment, saddling up and preparing to ride back to their first hideout to bring their things back.

151

O'Brien stopped behind an aspen, which afforded him cover. He was only thirty yards from the cabin now. And he was in his element. He had been stalking prey most of his life. You must emulate the cougar. You don't reveal your presence until you're close enough to strike. You blend in with your environment. You practice motionlessness. You wait for your opportunity. Then you strike quickly and with power.

He had followed all those rules when he approached a herd. Sometimes actually crawling on his belly, just like the big cat.

He reached to the soft dirt at his feet, and took a small handful and smeared it onto the barrel of the Winchester, so it would not glisten in the bright sun and attract their attention. He threw his Stetson on to the ground because it might occlude vision.

He took a deep breath in.

He was ready.

He didn't move directly to the front of the cabin. Because of the window there, which could expose him to view, he walked two legs of a triangle to get there. As he approached, he heard some soft noises where Guthrie and St Clair were saddling up. But the noises were coming at him directly through the cabin from its open windows, so he judged it to be coming from inside.

He was at the cabin away from the window, wondering if he should attempt to go at them from outside through that window. But then deciding he would go on in, because that assault seemed more certain of success.

He moved silently over to the front door, which just had a latch that kept it closed. He listened for more sounds, but there were none.

He stepped back to kick the door in, Winchester at the ready. Every fiber in him tensed for attack.

St Clair suddenly appeared around the corner of the cabin, heading for the door.

They both just stood there for a moment that seemed an eternity. No word spoken. Not a muscle moving.

Then, swift as lightning and equally deadly, St Clair drew and fired the right-hand Colt Army, exploding the tranquillity of that still photo moment and clubbing O'Brien in the chest with fiery hot lead.

O'Brien had not been positioned to face his unexpected adversary, and was struck just as he began raising the rifle to fire. Now he stumbled backward over uneven ground, lost balance, and fell, hitting the ground hard just in front of the door.

A slow grin came on to St Clair's lean face. Behind the cabin, Guthrie heard the shot but was behind his mount, starting to mount. He now disengaged himself slowly, with a deep frown.

Out front, O'Brien was hurting badly. But he knew it wasn't over. He still had the rifle alongside him, and as he saw St Clair approach him, decided to use a strategy taught to him by the Lakota. He lay very quietly, encouraging St Clair to come all the way.

In the next moment, St Clair was there. 'Too bad, hunter. Better luck next life.' He raised the Colt again, and aimed it at O'Brien's face.

153

O'Brien quickly raised the muzzle of the Winchester and fired without aiming. The big gun roared in the clearing, and the lead struck St Clair under the chin, traveled entirely through his skull, and blew the crown of his head away.

St Clair was frowning down at O'Brien as if responding to an insult, his jaw working with nothing coming out. Then he was on the ground, his left leg jumping there for a moment in reflex. He had been dead while still standing.

Now Wade Guthrie's head appeared in the window above O'Brien. He shouted an expletive, crimson-faced, and took a quick shot through the window that missed O'Brien's head by an inch. But as O'Brien raised the Winchester again, Guthrie's face disappeared.

O'Brien looked down at his wound. It was very high on his chest, by his shoulder. St Clair had shot too quickly, which was typical of many gunslingers. He got to his feet awkwardly, looking into the cabin through the window. But then he heard a sound from out the back. Through his new pain he walked to the corner of the cabin just in time to see Guthrie mounted and riding away, going past O'Brien to his right. O'Brien raised the long gun, but Guthrie had now cleverly slipped over on to the far side of his mount, partially off his saddle. Something he, too, had learned from the Indians, probably the Apache.

O'Brien did not have a clear shot at him. So he aimed carefully at the horse's head and fired.

Guthrie's horse plummeted to the ground with Guthrie aboard.

Guthrie had made it halfway to the protection of a stand of aspens, and lay with his horse about fifty yards away. The horse had fallen on him, and he was pinned underneath its flank, only his upper chest and head showing.

O'Brien was feeling the pain badly now. But as usual he ignored it, as he had ignored it when he had been trampled by stampeding buffalo. Or when the appaloosa had thrown him off in panic and broke his leg. He walked slowly over to Guthrie. Partway there Guthrie worked the Schofield loose from its holster and took a wild shot at O'Brien, and struck him a grazing blow on the neck.

O'Brien didn't even break stride. When he got there, Guthrie aimed the revolver again, more carefully. O'Brien raised the Winchester again and it roared out a last time, beating Guthrie by a fractional second and violently striking him in center chest, just over his horse's back.

Guthrie's eyes saucered in quick shock, and then he was staring malevolently at O'Brien. 'You wrecked all of it,' he gasped out raggedly. Then, in a croaking voice: 'The rest – is silence.'

O'Brien stared down at his lifeless figure. It was over.

'You shouldn't have burnt my cabin,' he growled out.

That seemed to say it all.

At that same time in Birney Pass, Sarah had been facing her own crisis. For the past hour her muffled cries of pain had been coming from her closed bedroom, while Ethan Purvis slumped tensely on a soft chair with his crutch and Dru paced the room like an expectant father. Now, as they listened, her cries had ceased and there was a new sound, of a healthy baby crying out its protests to its suddenly new world.

Dru turned to her husband. 'My God! Did you hear that!'

Purvis was grinning widely. 'She did it, Dru!'

In the next moment the doctor came out from the bedroom with a tired smile on his weathered face. 'It's a boy, folks.'

'Oh, thank God,' Dru sighed. 'They both wanted that.'

'He weighs almost ten pounds,' the doctor told them, shaking his head. 'I don't know how she kept that in her. This boy O'Brien must be a big-sized fellow.'

'That ain't the half of it,' Dru rejoined drily. 'Say, how's our girl, Doc?' With a new solemnity.

'I'm pleased to report that she took it very nicely,' he smiled. 'She's already holding her red-faced offspring. I reckon I was wrong about Olivia. She probably helped with all of that midwife chicanery.'

'Can we see her?' Dru asked him.

'Give her a few minutes with her new treasure, then go on in,' he said. He was finished drying his hands off. 'In the meantime I'll leave you for a while. I got a leg to set down the street. I'll check in on her this evening.'

The doctor left then, just as Olivia came from the bedroom carrying the baby. It was all cleaned up and wrapped in a light blanket.

'Well, here he is. Sarah said to bring him out to you. Ain't he a beauty?'

The boy was big, all right, and very alert. Already he seemed to be focusing on things. Dru took him carefully, privately wanting one just like him. 'He's just darling,' she said softly. 'Is Sarah decent?'

'She's ready for company now, I think. Go on in. I'm leaving.'

Dru carried Sarah's little O'Brien into the bedroom, and Sarah greeted her with a big smile. She still looked lovely, but very tired.

'What do you think?' she said quietly. 'Did I really do that?'

'He's the most beautiful thing in Birney Pass,' Dru smiled.

'O'Brien will be so pleased,' Sarah said. Then her pretty face went somber. 'I can't enjoy the moment as much, Dru. Because I don't know about him.'

Dru sighed heavily. 'I know, honey.'

That afternoon and evening passed comfortably for Sarah, who slept for most of the time. She had a cup of broth at suppertime, and then slept some more. The baby, not yet named because of O'Brien's absence, was put in the Purvises' bedroom for a while. In mid-evening Sarah woke, was told the child was sleeping, and joined Dru and Purvis in the parlor with Dru's help. The doctor had looked in earlier and told Sarah she was doing just fine and could get out of bed if she wished.

Now the three of them were sitting in the parlor, with Sarah propped up on the long sofa.

'I can't sleep any longer. I keep waking up and wondering where he is. And if I'll ever see him again.'

Neither one of them knew what to say. They had the same doubts now as Sarah.

'I know one thing,' Purvis told her. 'He's the best man with a gun I ever met.'

Sarah gave him a half-smile.

'I just feel real optimistic,' Dru said with bravado. 'I got this feeling. And I been known to see things. I think that hunter will adapt to town life, eventually take Ethan's job when he quits it, and that youngster in there will grow up big and smart and end up senator or governor in our new state.' A small laugh.

Sarah looked past them to a window. 'Governor,' she said quietly, and seriously.

They exchanged an approving grin.

'O'Brien. A good name for politics,' Purvis offered. 'I think—'

But a neighbor boy's voice came from the street. 'Sheriff! You got a visitor!'

They all exchanged curious looks, and Sarah's heart suddenly was thumping her chest.

Outside, O'Brien was dismounting awkwardly, his left arm in a sling hastily applied over a thick bandage that covered a through-and-through wound from St Clair's revolver. There was also a small bandage on his neck where Guthrie had grazed him, done by a Culver Junction doctor. He walked tiredly to the porch, where Purvis met him.

Purvis was grinning from ear to ear. 'O'Brien.'

'Purvis. What happened to you?'

'It's a long story.' He saw the sling. 'What about Guthrie?'

'Oh. You won't be hearing from him no more.'

Inside, Sarah had gotten a glimpse of her husband, and a heavy weight lifted off her chest. 'Oh, my God, Dru. He's back. He's really back.'

Dru had tears in her eyes. She turned to Sarah. 'Now, get that face off, honey. Show him how happy you are.'

Sarah wiped at an eye. 'Help me up, Dru. I want to greet him standing.'

Purvis had just assured O'Brien that Sarah had gotten through her pregnancy all right, and that she had delivered him a son. O'Brien just stood silent for a moment. 'Jesus.'

A moment later he was inside, and when he saw Sarah standing there, looking as lovely as he remembered her, something happened to him that never had before. He felt a choking up in his throat, and a welling of emotion that was entirely new to him.

He walked over to her. She was looking at the sling. 'Oh, God. You're hurt.'

159

'It ain't nothing. The doc says it will come off in a couple weeks. I figure a few days.'

She leaned against him, laying her head on his broad shoulder. 'I worried so much that you wouldn't return.'

'I hear you give me a little something,' he grinned.

'Just what you wanted,' she told him. 'And he looks like you. He's in the next room.'

They went in there together, with Sarah feeling much stronger now that O'Brien was back.

'There he is,' Sarah said. 'All yours.'

The baby was coming awake. O'Brien knelt beside the bed, and touched the small hand, and it grabbed his finger.

He grinned, a rarity for him. 'I'll be damned.'

He rose, and turned to Sarah, and she kissed him softly.

'He's already got grit. He might get anything he wants,' O'Brien suggested. 'He might be a damn cattle baron some day.'

Dru had come in behind them. Sarah glanced at her. 'Or governor,' she smiled.

'Why not?' O'Brien agreed. 'Even a governor.'

Sarah was happier than she had ever been. O'Brien, she was certain now, would gradually accept a tamer lifestyle, and they would become a part of a community. And a little later, she would see to it that their son had a chance to be a leader of that community as he watched his father's emergence from the wilds into a more civilized world.

It didn't seem too much to ask.